**In a low voice Drake said, "Two can play the same game."**

She rolled to her side. Her gaze locked with his. "Do you really want to play?"

Drake climbed out of bed and looked at her. "I'm leaving. You're staying."

"You didn't answer my question."

"Which one? Do I want you? Yes. You are the most sexy woman I've ever seen. The most amazing one. The bravest. The most beautiful. Hell yeah, I want you."

"You mean that?" Did he really feel that way? No one had ever said anything close to that to her before.

He looked into her eyes. "Every word of it."

Trice slipped from the bed not caring about the skimpy clothing she wore. She walked to Drake, then put her arms around his neck and kissed him. "Thank you for that. No one has ever said anything like that to me."

Dear Reader,

I spent a wonderful week cruising around Iceland and loved it enough to want to revisit it while writing a book. I hope you enjoy your visit to Iceland through my story as much as I did.

You know, it's funny the turns that life takes, often ending up in the wrong place at the right time or the reverse. That's what happens to Trice and Drake. One is coming to town and the other is leaving. Life is just letting them have a taste of each other then snatching them away. Can lovers build a lifetime on just a few days of pleasure?

I love to hear from my readers. I can be reached at Susan@SusanCarlisle.com.

*Susan*

**Susan Carlisle**'s love affair with books began when she made a bad grade in mathematics. Not allowed to watch TV until the grade had improved, she filled her time with books. Turning her love of reading into a love for writing romance, she pens hot medicals. She loves castles, traveling, afternoon tea, reading voraciously and hearing from her readers. Join her newsletter at susancarlisle.com.

## Books by Susan Carlisle

### Harlequin Medical Romance

#### *Atlanta Children's Hospital*

*Mending the ER Doc's Heart*
*Reunited with the Children's Doc*
*Wedding Date with Her Best Friend*
*Second Chance for the Heart Doctor*

#### *Kentucky Derby Medics*

*Falling for the Trauma Doc*
*An Irish Vet in Kentucky*

*Pacific Paradise, Second Chance*
*The Single Dad's Holiday Wish*
*Reunited with Her Daredevil Doc*
*Taming the Hot-Shot Doc*
*From Florida Fling to Forever*

Visit the Author Profile page
at Harlequin.com for more titles.

To Finnley

One of the greatest pleasures in my life.

# CHAPTER ONE

A KNOT HUNG in Beatrice Shell's throat. She searched the land below for the town that should be at the end of the northern Iceland fjord. The stretch of blue water grew closer as the pilot of the single-engine plane prepared to land. Ahead she could just make out a single runway of black asphalt with piles of gray stone alongside it, extending into the water. She'd never seen anything like it. Yet that wasn't a huge surprise. Coming to Iceland had been her first real trip anywhere.

The large airliner she had taken to Reykjavík had been scary, but exciting at the same time. Getting into the small plane had created a different sensation all together. Terror. The six-seater plane was nothing like the jet, the only similarity being it soared through the air. This flight had kept her hair standing on end and her heart palpitating in her chest. She would see if there was a boat out when she left. No more swooping and dipping for her. Small plane transportation wasn't her idea of a good time.

Her fingers gripped the well-worn seat as the wings tipped one way, then the other. The pilot lined up with the runway. If he missed it, he would put them in the water. She glanced at the beautiful snowcapped mountains and shivered. Into the cold water.

She brushed her finger across the small scar on the top of her hand, then forced herself to open her eyelids. Isn't this what she'd been wanting to do since she'd learned of her rare skin disorder as a teen? To have a connection. Belong.

She'd experienced a blistering skin rash. Her foster mother had taken her to the doctor. After much discussion and other doctors being called in for their opinions, she had learned she had a skin disease called hepatoerythropoietic por-phyria disease or HEP. What intrigued her the most about the disease was it was genetic, par-ticular to people with Nordic ancestry. Until then she'd had no hint of her background.

She recovered completely with little scarring from the flare-up of the disease. She would al-ways carry the gene, but the illness would be-come nothing more unless she spent too much time in the sun or was prescribed the wrong drugs. The positive thing that came out of the experience was the knowledge of her Nordic lineage. When she had saved enough money, she'd had a DNA test done, which had led her to Iceland.

With a squeak of tires, the plane touched the asphalt, bounced, then settled to coast to a stop. She let out the breath she'd been holding. At least they weren't in the water.

When the opportunity arose to work in a clinic in Iceland for a year, she'd applied for the chance. She was tickled when she won the position. Now she could care for people with the same genetic background as herself. They might not be direct family, but they were closer than anyone else she had known.

She dared a look out the window. Another plane sat parked in front of a white block building, and they coasted beside it. The sign on the wall read Welcome to Seydisfjordur.

Gathering her purse and her small duffel bag, Trice climbed out of the side door the pilot had opened. He offered his hand, and she accepted it. The last thing she needed was to arrive at her new job with a busted nose from falling on her face. That wouldn't encourage the town's faith in her medical abilities.

She glanced around at the buildings lining a single road following the curve of the fjord. The town was located in the end of a narrow green valley. A gentle-looking river lead into the mouth of the fjord. The backs of the town structures hovered against a wall of rock creating the fjord. In the sunshine, the stores and houses glowed white, pink, yellow and light blue with a few having red roofs. If anything, the place was picture-perfect.

Her heart beat faster. She'd dream of coming this far north for years but never thought it would happen. Now she was here. This place she could call home. Excitement built. This could be her chance to find a link to family. No matter how distant.

"Miss, your suitcase is right here. The clinic is over there." The man pointed around the water toward the only piece of land wide enough to have a center street with buildings on both sides. "It's the white building with the red cross sign."

"Thank you." She pulled the handle up on her case, assuming she was expected to walk the half a mile. She was thankful for her warm socks and her down vest. Her new hiking boots maybe not so much. They had been a going away gift from her best friend, Andrea. "I appreciate the ride in."

The man with a beard lifted and lowered his chin and went back to the plane.

Taking the suitcase handle, she rolled it toward the small terminal building that sat securely on land. At least this part of the airport wasn't surrounded by water. Unable to see a red cross from that distance, she followed the road toward the village.

The sun shone bright, and the air was brisk. Thankfully the place wasn't covered in snow.

People often mixed Greenland up with Iceland. Greenland was icy and Iceland was green.

Trice had been offered the job at the last minute because another doctor had backed out. She'd jumped at the opportunity despite the short notice. In less than forty-eight hours, she'd wrapped up her personal business, stored her few belongings and stepped on a plane bound for the far-off north. Andrea had thought she was crazy and wished her well.

She had not even had a chance to break in her new boots between yesterday and today. After a hurried last two days, a long plane ride, and the altitude, she didn't care much about the time zone changes.

Trice surveyed the area past the airport away from town. In that direction, there was some type of business located in a large red metal building next to the water. Just how much could happen in this tiny place? Compared to living in metropolitan Atlanta, where she'd spent her entire life, this town was no larger than a neighborhood. No doubt she would have culture shock. She wasn't sure if that would be a good thing or a bad thing. She was too busy trying to keep her mind off the ache of her toes to worry about how she would make this work.

Around the curve of the bay, she saw the white clapboard house. Outside it hung a small sign with the red cross on it. She headed that way.

Trudging on, she promised herself with every step she would remove her boots as soon as she had a chance. The impeccable view of the vibrantly painted wooden buildings, the vivid blue water, the green of the valley, and the white of the snowcapped mountain filled her. Here she had a chance to find her lineage and through that herself. She could feel that in her bones, just not her toes.

Drake Stevansson noticed the woman for two reasons. First, he didn't know her. Having been born and raised in Seydisfjordur, he knew everyone. Second, even from a distance, something about the woman intrigued him. Maybe it was her vivid-colored yellow coat or the hot pink suitcase she pulled. Whatever it was, she was eye-catching.

She followed the long curve of the road into town. He handed the envelope to his aunt, the postmistress, and started in the stranger's direction and toward the medical clinic. What could possibly land this fascinating creature here? He had seen plenty of people come from a cruise ship, but there wasn't one in port. She must have been on the plane.

The woman continued on but slower now. She had a rather haggard look. Every once in a while, she stopped and shook a foot. What was that about? The road wasn't muddy. Did she walk like that all the time?

She would square her shoulders, raise her chin and start again. Something about this woman screamed, "I won't be defeated." That spoke to him. That was an Icelandic mantra. His gut said she had the determination, the grit needed to live through so many hours of darkness in the winter, not to mention the cold. Why that should matter to him he had no idea. He would be leaving soon with the possibility of not returning except to visit.

As a boy, he had watched his grandfather die because there wasn't anyone close who could do a simple appendectomy. He'd promised himself then that he would become a surgeon. He would fix people's bodies. He had gotten far enough in his training that he could do the procedures, but he still need the practice hours. He had been working on those when he was called away.

Drake had returned to Seydisfjordur for the funeral of his mentor and friend, Dr. Johannsson, to learn there was no one to oversee the practice. Drake had made arrangements for a break from his surgery work so he could provide the town medical care. Locating someone to take his place had turned into a frustrating ordeal. Finally, someone had agreed to come for a year. The mayor had taken almost two years to find someone. The man was expected any day. The mayor would continue to look for someone else beyond that. In two more weeks, after settling the new person in, Drake would leave.

The only issue tugging at him not to go was Luce. She was getting older, frailer. Because of circumstances, he had become responsible for her. Yet she encouraged him leaving. "Don't worry about me. Go follow your dream." The new doctor had better be good enough to care for Luce.

Drake reached the medical clinic. He stood outside and watched the woman approach. She made the same actions once again with her feet before she reached him.

Her look focused on him as she crossed the short distance. He found her even more interesting up close. Her blond hair was as fair as any person he knew. She controlled it by twisting it on the back of her head with a sparkling hair clip. She wore a bright red shirt, baggy black pants, and had a yellow, red, orange and black scarf around her neck. An orange bag was slung over her shoulder. Everything about her screamed confidence.

"Hello. Can I help you?"

She came to a stop in front of him, again lifted a foot and shook it from side to side "Oh, good, you speak English. I'm afraid my Icelandic is nonexistent."

"You are in luck. I happen to be one of the

ninety-eight percent of the people who speak English in Iceland. I'm going to use it now." Drake leaned down so they were at eye level. He wished he could see her eyes, but they were covered by sunglasses. "Are you okay? Lost? How can I help you?"

"My feet hurt. New boots." She moaned.

With a compassionate smile, he said, "I've been there. I can help with that."

"That's okay. I just need to get them off. Mind if I sit on your step?" She was already moving to do so.

"Not at all."

She pushed the pull handle of the case down. "I just need to get my tennis shoes out." She moved to picked up the bag.

"Let me have that." Drake lifted the case. "Come inside. You'll be more comfortable here."

"Thanks. I appreciate that." She followed him inside the small wooden building. She flopped into one of the plastic chairs in the waiting room with a sigh, resting her feet on her heels.

"Here, let me help." Drake went down on his haunches.

"You don't need to do that." She pulled her feet back.

He looked into her blue eyes that reminded him of the fjord with the sun shining across it. When the few other single men in town found out about her, they would be scrambling to her door.

He wouldn't be around long enough to do that. Something about this woman made him suspect he would be missing out. He reached for her foot and began unlacing the boot. "I'm a doctor. It's my job to help those who hurt."

"So you are the doctor here." Her look met his as she studied him.

"I am for at least another two weeks."

She winced as he removed her footwear.

He dropped the boot to the floor. "Easy. You must have really done some damage to your feet."

She wiggled her foot. "That at least feels better, but I have no desire to put another shoe on."

"Let's remove the sock and see what's going on." He slowly rolled the sock off. Her foot was red and swollen with blisters on both sides. "You did a job."

"I should've known better. But they were a gift, and I wanted to wear them when my friend was the one taking me to the airport." She lifted her foot with the intent of rubbing it.

"Don't do that. Then it will really hurt. Wait right here. I have just what you need." He stood.

"I'd rather take care of them myself," she called after him.

"As the medical professional here, I'd rather you let me make sure you're okay." He headed down the hall without giving her time to respond.

Soon he returned with a square plastic container and Epsom salts. He poured a generous amount of salt into the pan.

She pushed a straight length of hair that had escaped her clip away from her face. "I can do this at the place where I am staying."

He gave her a direct look. "You can't even walk there. Let me at least get you comfortable enough to do that. I'll get the warm water."

"If you insist." She grinned.

He glanced back at her. "I do. Around here we take any injury seriously. If it gets out of hand, we have a long way to go to get treatment."

When he came back this time, she had the other boot and sock off and was leaning back in her chair with a look of acceptance.

He poured the water into the pan. "Ease your feet in. You don't want them burned on top of being blistered."

She dipped an unpolished big toe of a slim, delicate foot into the water with a sigh. Slowly her feet went into the liquid. "This feels wonderful. Thank you."

"You keep those in there for a few minutes. I'll be back with a towel." He returned with a bottle of oil. He poured a generous amount into the water.

"What's that? It smells good." She inhaled.

Drake watched her neck lengthen. He was tempted to run a finger down the length of the smooth, creamy skin. "It is something I mix myself. It's fish oil with some local herbs. I use it when hikers come by for help. We get a number of those this time of year."

"So this isn't your first time to help out like this." She fluttered her feet in the water.

"No, I see abused feet more than I'd like to."

She curled her toes. "This will be the last time you will see mine."

He took the chair beside her. "Famous last words."

She leaned back beside him. "This is amazing."

He liked this flamboyant woman's attitude. "Do you have some nice warm socks and some substantial shoes that are not brand-new?"

She nodded. "I've got my tennis shoes in my suitcase, but the thought of putting them on makes my feet hurt even more."

"I have something you can wear that will make your feet happier." Drake went to his office and located the soft boots his grandmother had given him for Christmas. He had brought them to the clinic thinking he might like to wear them when he was doing paperwork. Finally, he would be putting them to good use. He added a pair of clean socks.

This time he found the woman with her head back and eyes closed. Was she asleep?

Seconds later her eyelids opened.

He handed her the socks. "These are made of

natural fibers and will help your feet avoid getting infected." He placed the boots beside the pan.

She sat straighter. With a hand, she pushed another stray strand of hair away from her face. Raising her chin, she looked at him. "You know, I don't even know your name."

He offered his hand. "I'm Dr. Stevansson. Drake."

She jerked to an upright position. "You are? Well, now I'm completely embarrassed."

"Why?"

"Because I'm here to take your place. I'm Dr. Beatrice Shell."

That he hadn't expected. She would be his replacement. He should've thought of it first thing, but nothing about her looked—he glanced at her petite build and soft face, then her flashy clothes—like someone he would expect to live in Iceland. Or that would survive a Seydisfjordur winter. And he'd been told by the mayor that a man had been hired for the doctor position.

Drake had stayed out of the search process for his replacement, both by his own choice and the mayor's. Drake had feared that if he was involved, he would never think anyone was qualified enough to have the position. The mayor's reasoning was that since Drake didn't care enough to stay, he shouldn't have a say in who took his place.

"But I guess I'm at the right place," Beatrice said, "and you are just the person I was looking for."

Drake liked that idea too much. Still, she was coming, and he was going. Nothing would be happening between them. Just his luck. The first woman near his age and not related to him who had shown up in town in years and he'd be leaving soon.

She offered him her hand. "I'm Trice to my friends. I was expecting somebody much older."

He chuckled. "I get that quite a lot." In fact, he heard it enough for it to grate on his nerves. Dr. Johannsson had been the town doctor for years. He'd delivered Drake and most of the adults in town. Compared to him, Drake was young.

Drake had worked for Dr. Johannsson as a teen and through high school, then gone off to medical school. The old doctor had encouraged Drake to consider taking over the practice, but Drake's dream was surgery. He felt like he could help more people using those skills. But it meant leaving Luce, which he didn't like doing. She had no intention of moving from her home. Unfortunately, there was no surgery clinic near Seydisfjordur. That was an entirely different issue.

He gave Trice a good long look. No, he hadn't expected this woman with her sassy attitude, flashy clothing, and full-of-confidence outlook. She appealed to him, too much so. The last woman he'd liked couldn't leave Seydisfjordur fast enough. Trice acted thrilled she was there. "I was expecting…a man."

Her shoulders went back at that statement. "Women now make up more than fifty percent of doctors." Her brows drew together. "No one told you? The doctor who was coming backed out at the last minute. I only found out I had the job a couple of days ago."

He hadn't been told on purpose would be his guess. Drake put his hands up in defense. "That wasn't a sexist statement. It's just that we don't get many women who want to live in such a distant and hostile environment. I'm just surprised, that's all."

"I'm tougher than I look." Determination showed clear in her eyes.

His mouth quirked. "You'll need to be."

Yes, he liked this woman who seemed excited about being in his hometown. Would she still feel that way this winter? What was she looking for? Or running from? Too bad he wouldn't be around long enough to find out.

Trice gingerly put her feet on the towel Drake had placed on the floor. "Now that I have thoroughly embarrassed myself, could you point me in the direction of where I'll be staying?"

"I'll do better than that. I'll show you. I'm sure you are tired."

She chuckled. "Yeah, that would be an under-statement. After two plane changes and then a prop plane to get here, I could use a rest."

"Where did you start out from?"

"Atlanta."

He whistled. "Bright lights, big city. Seydis-fjordur will be a big change for you."

"So far it looks wonderful." Her eyes were glowing with anticipation. "I can hardly wait to get to know everyone."

"It won't take you long. Many will line up to see you."

That she wasn't used to. Most of her life she had gone unnoticed. It would be nice to have people actually want to meet her. She pulled on the soft, thick socks. With some trepidation, she pushed her foot into the first shoe. It felt wonderful around her abused toes. With less concern, she did the same with the other foot. "Thank you. I dreaded putting on even my tennis shoes. I promise to return them all clean."

"It's not a problem." He stood.

"I'm sure the last few minutes make me look unqualified to take over here, but I promise to have my act together tomorrow."

"Everybody makes mistakes about footwear at times. I certainly have." He smiled.

Trice doubted he had made any mistakes. He looked and sounded like the perfect guy. Kind, understanding, gentle, caring, and best of all, male. Too bad he would be leaving. Something about Drake made her believe he was different from the last guy she had dated. She stood and hobbled toward her suitcase. For some reason, she sensed this man was careful with women's hearts.

"I'll get that. You can hardly make it to the door. You can't handle the case too."

She managed to get down the steps only by holding the rail with two hands.

Drake quickly came up behind her. He placed her case on the ground, then bent in front of her. "Get on."

"You have to be kidding. You can't mean to carry me through the street on your back!" She couldn't think of a less dignified way of making a first impression than parading through town on this man's back.

"Would you rather be cradled in my arms?"

Her pride refused to let him do that.

He looked over his shoulder. "If I don't carry you, how do you plan to get there?"

She glanced around.

Drake's look held hers. "You could stay here at the clinic if you wanted."

She considered sleeping on the examination table after having been on an airplane the better part of the day. The idea didn't appeal. "Okay."

"Wrap your arms around my neck. It's just a couple houses down."

She did as he said. His arms looped under her

knees. Her front pressed against his back. Heat washed through her. This was far too familiar for someone she didn't even know, but what choice did she have? Walking wasn't a good suggestion.

He pulled the handle up on her suitcase and took off at a steady stride.

She voiced next to his ear, "I can get my suitcase later."

"I believe I can handle both of you at one time. Neither of you is very heavy." He threw the words over his shoulder without any exertion indicated in his voice.

Trice couldn't help but appreciate the movement of his muscles as he walked. His broad shoulders made her confident he wouldn't drop her. This was a man who knew how to care for people and took pleasure in doing so.

They made their way down the road lined with houses and businesses no taller than two floors. Curious faces met them along the way. A few people stepped out of the buildings to watch them.

"Is everyone going to know?" She started to hide her face but thought better of it.

"Pretty much. There are only around one thousand people who live in this area, and most of them are related to me. I would bet that in an hour, everyone will have heard of your arrival."

"Good to know." She smiled at one of the ladies, who waved.

He chuckled.

People continued to stare. A few spoke to Drake as they went. He responded with a grin in return.

One older man joined in beside Drake and asked, "Who you got there?"

"The new doctor. You can meet her later. We're kind of busy right now."

The man glanced at her. "Why is she on your back?"

Trice buried her face in his shoulder. She felt more than heard Drake's laugher. His body shook.

"Isn't she a little old to need to ride that way?" The man sounded perplexed.

"Gustaf, we'll talk about it later."

Trice groaned as Drake moved on. "I'm going to have to work extra hard to earn people's respect after this show."

"You'll find people here are warm and forgiving." He stopped in front of a pink house trimmed in white.

He set the case to the side then let her legs go. She slid down his back. Heat she'd not felt in a long time washed through her. Mercy, the man had a nice body. She'd had one serious relationship, but his body wasn't as defined as Drake's.

Nor had been his strength of will. Her ex had been from a society family, and his mother made it clear Trice's background was not suitable. A foster child with no family would never do. Her boyfriend couldn't stand up to his mother, so he and Trice parted ways. A marriage between them probably wouldn't have worked anyway. Her sense of adventure and sense of humor hadn't always been appreciated. Her boyfriend had been far too serious. Worse, he had been under his family's thumb. Trice wanted a man who stood on his own two feet.

Even with her and Drake's short association, she didn't think those were issues for him. But she shouldn't be making these observations. She had no interest in becoming involved in a relationship. She wouldn't take the chance on being second choice again. There had been enough of that in her life.

Something about Drake appealed to her. Maybe it was the fact he had been willing to carry her as he had. He seemed to enjoy the absurdity in life.

Drake's strong grip held her arm, letting her get her feet under her. He knocked on the door but didn't wait for an answer before he opened it. "Luce?"

The scrape of chair legs and shuffling of feet came from the back of the house. He carried the luggage inside. She followed, closing the door behind her. A petite stoop-shouldered woman with a weathered face entered.

"Drake, what do you mean coming into my home bellowing?" The woman's voice was gruff but held a tender note.

"I'm sorry, Luce. I brought your new boarder. This is Dr. Shell."

The woman, who must have been close to a century old, gave Trice a long look. "From America, I hear."

"Yes ma'am, I am." Was that a good or bad thing?

"Nice manners too."

Somehow Trice believed that was high praise. "Thank you. It's nice to meet you. I appreciate you giving me a place to stay."

"You have come to take my Drake's place."

There was a tone of sadness to that question. "I have come to take care of the people here for a year and do some research."

The older woman studied Trice a moment, her eyes landing on her feet. "She is wearing your Christmas present." Her accusing look shifted to Drake.

"She is. By the way, Luce is my grandmother." Drake hung his head as if in shame.

Trice liked the idea a man as large as Drake could be intimidated by this tiny woman. She had certainly called him on the carpet.

"She's just borrowing them. I had them over at the office to wear if my feet were cold while I was doing paperwork. Dr. Shell's feet hurt."

"They are very nice," Trice assured the woman. "Thank you…" She looked at Drake.

"You may call me Luce. Everyone does." The

woman gave a sharp nod and said to Trice, "I'll show you where you will stay."

Trice, with Drake carrying her case, followed the older woman through the small, dim home and out the back door. In the backyard stood an even smaller cottage.

Luce opened the door. "You have everything you need in here except a full kitchen. There is a microwave and a toaster oven, but if you want to do more, you're welcome to use my kitchen anytime you please. All you have to do is to come in the back door."

Luce pushed the cottage door open. "Come in and I'll show you around."

Trice joined her. Drake entered behind her, setting the case out of the way. With him there, the place went from small to tiny. After that ride on his back, she was too aware of him. He seemed to surround her.

Luce explained everything in detail. Which wasn't much. A solid wooden bed sat in one corner. In another was a bookshelf filled with books, a chair and small table with a floor lamp beside it. Nearby rested a TV on a substantial-looking dresser with drawers. Across from that side of the room was a kitchen area that consisted of a cabinet, a table and two chairs. A small bath took up the back corner. A hoop rug created out of pastel colors lay on the floor.

As far as Trice was concerned, she'd found

heaven. After growing up with little she could call her own, this would be a treat. "This really looks wonderful. I know I'll enjoy staying here."

"If you need anything, you just ask me or tell Drake. He helps take care of things around here when he's not busy seeing patients." The old woman flashed him a look. "At least, until he leaves."

"Luce, you said you wanted me to go. To be happy." He put an arm around the woman's shoulders, looking at her with a teasing grin.

"I do want you to follow your dream. I will miss you. Enough of that. You aren't gone yet. Let's let the girl settle in." She nudged him toward the door.

Drake went while looking over his shoulder at Trice. "See how I'm treated around here? No wonder I want to return to my work in London."

That far away? Why did that idea bother her? She had just met the man. Those thoughts she must squelch. They led to disappointment and pain.

"When you get ready for a tour of the clinic, you come on over. I'll be there until five o'clock. Better yet, why don't we just let that wait until in the morning?"

"Thanks for your help and for letting me borrow your shoes. And of course for the ride."

He grinned. "My pleasure."

It had been hers as well.

# CHAPTER TWO

DRAKE LOOKED UP from his paperwork when the door of the clinic opened early the next morning. He saw Trice's blond hair before the rest of her. His heart did a little dip and jerk before it settled. Something about the woman charmed him. Why here and why now? He needed to keep his interest under control. There wasn't time for them to get involved. It wouldn't be fair to either of them if they did.

"Good morning," he offered as she closed the door. He pushed away from his desk that sat in the small area doubling as a waiting room.

"Hey." She looked around the area as if taking in all the details.

"How'd you sleep last night?"

"Good," she said as if in afterthought, her attention still on the space.

"I'm not surprised after the day you had." He stood. Once again she was dressed in a vivid colors. Her shirt was sunshine yellow, paired with jeans. Her hair was pulled on top of her head and bound by a piece of cloth the same shade as her shirt.

She fingered the sign-in clipboard. "I appreciate the coffee and pastry. That was very sweet of you."

"I just figured after the day you had yesterday, you wouldn't bother with buying food."

"It was nice to wake to a hot cup of coffee waiting. Along with the wake-up knock."

His chest expanded with pleasure. He felt overly pleased she had been glad to receive his gift.

She looked down the hall. "I'm ready for the tour. I need to appear professional when someone comes in after yesterday. I should try to redeem myself some."

"You have nothing to be embarrassed about." He had to have fielded at least thirty questions about that show. On the phone and in person.

"I think that piggyback ride through the middle of town might qualify under embarrassment. Too close to a Lady Godiva ride."

He chuckled. "Except you were fully clothed."

She grinned. "Thank goodness."

Drake liked she didn't take herself too seriously. He enjoyed this woman a little too much for comfort, especially since he would be leaving. His life had been on hold for so long that it felt good to trade quips with Trice. "How're your feet this morning? Do I need to give them a look?"

"They are fine. Thanks. I'm even returning your shoes." She held them up by two fingers.

"I would tell you that you are welcome to keep them, but I would suffer the wrath of Luce."

She smiled. "We can't have that."

He took the shoes from her. "Come on. I'll give the half-cent tour while I put these away. You'll know where they are if you need them."

"You're not taking them with you when you go?"

He started down the hall. "Nope. I won't need them. It's much warmer in London."

"So, what is it you're going to London for?" She slowly followed him, stopping to glance into the rooms they passed.

"I'm returning to surgery training." Drake could hardly wait. He had missed it.

"What happened, you didn't finish?" She sounded genuinely interested.

"Dr. Johannsson died. I returned for his funeral and didn't go back." He just couldn't leave.

"Why not?"

He stopped and looked at her. "After Dr. Johannsson died, the town needed a doctor. I couldn't leave them without medical care. It has taken the mayor two years to find someone to replace me. By the way, why did you decide to come here, of all places?"

"Because I've wanted to come to Iceland for years. I'm also interested in researching HEP."

His brows narrowed. "That answer I hadn't expected. Hepatoerythropoietic porphyria is an interesting condition for an American to study. Why that of all things?"

"Because I carry the gene."

His brows rose. "Really? So your family is from here?"

"My DNA test says Iceland, and other Scandinavian countries by smaller degrees."

"What have your parents told you?"

"Nothing. I went into foster care when I was three. I remember little about my mother and never knew my father. I was too young to remember anything my mother might have said. Which I doubt she did. I understand she died of a drug overdose when I was five."

His eyes filled with sympathy. "I'm so sorry."

Trice shrugged. "It is what it is. Before you ask, no, I wasn't adopted. People want babies, and I was almost six by then. It didn't happen for me. I was passed from foster home to foster home." She paused as if making a decision, then continued, "After I learned I had the HEP gene and it was explained to me how only certain people had it, I then started reading everything I could find on the subject. I made excellent grades, and that led me to medical school. I have a general medical degree, but I'm interested in research as well. I wanted to come here because it offered me a chance to do both."

Drake knew everyone in town and was related to most of them. The idea of not knowing his family was a foreign concept for him. The chance to be alone was part of the appeal of returning to London. Too often they had been involved in his business. "I didn't mean to pry."

She shrugged. "I had often wondered what my background was, and finding out I had HEP gave me a link."

He watched Trice. Her eyes had brightened. Then he understood. "You're looking for some bridge to your family."

"Yes. No. I don't know. I don't think I'll find my grandparents or anything like that, but I am interested in the people who share the disease with me."

The woman became more interesting by the minute. "That sounds reasonable. But patient care can keep you pretty busy around here."

"I can handle both. Patient care will always come first."

He liked hearing that. After all, these were his family and friends.

Trice looked at him. "You're having a hard time giving up being responsible, aren't you?"

Was he that transparent? He hung his head. "A little bit."

"That's understandable. I'm sure I will feel the same way when it's time for me to leave. It's natural."

Somehow this conversation wasn't making him feel any better. "Let me finish showing you around."

The tension in her body eased. "Thanks, I would like that."

"We aren't that busy on a daily basis. There are clinic days for regular checkups and days for shots. Otherwise there will be those who come in to see you with the usual illnesses. Then there are the emergencies. Which reminds me, I need to call the air ambulance about an issue."

"How are emergencies handled?" She looked around the examination room as if taking stock of where everything was stored.

"I stabilize the patient the best I can. If I can't handle it here, then I call the air ambulance. If the weather is fine, then a fixed-wing plane is dispatched. If the weather is bad, which is usually in the winter, then a helicopter will be used. In the worst-case scenario, a coast guard helicopter will be sent."

Drake couldn't help but be proud of the little clinic. He had made a number of improvements during his time. "Come along this way."

She started up the hall toward the front. "I did notice you have a couple of beds here where people can stay overnight."

"I do, but that happens rarely. Most wish to go home, and I stop in to see them." Many times he shared an evening meal with the patient's family.

"So you make house calls?"

"On occasion. I also do a monthly well-child clinic and another one for the geriatric patients. On those days, a nurse flies in to help."

"That sounds straightforward." She wandered into one of the two examination rooms.

He had to give her credit. She was self-assured if nothing else. Or was she just putting on an act. Where did she get all that confidence?

"Until it isn't." He stopped in front of the open door.

She followed him down a short hallway. Doors led off to the right side.

"Back here is a small kitchen, lab and supply room. You're welcome to bring in anything you like and set it up."

"A coffee machine is all I need." She looked into the cabinets.

"Got that, but if you need special beans or flavored syrups, you'll need to bring it. Plain Jane coffee is what I have here."

She looked at the setup. "I never developed a taste for the fancy drinks. There wasn't money for that. It looks like you stay well supplied for medical work. How often do you order?"

"Once a month. Supplies come in by ship. I'll show you where all that information is."

He started back up the hall, speaking over his shoulder. "We have telecommunication with the hospital. If we can't resolve problems here, then the ambulance is called. But as you can imagine, that's only as good as the weather allows."

Trice covertly studied the handsome, tall blond man with a shadow of a beard as he showed her around. His pride for the place was evident on his face. He looked like the Nordic Vikings whose blood ran through his veins. It didn't take much for her to imagine him standing on the front of his long boat, a foot on the gunwale, his hair flying in the wind as he led his men on a raid across the water to England. His chest would be thrust out beneath a breastplate, strong legs holding him steady. Everything about Drake said he was in control of his world.

She didn't need anybody in control of her world. After years of being told where to live and what to do, her life was finally her own to oversee. Now was the time for her to find herself and what she wanted. Where she belonged.

The door opened, taking her attention away from Drake. A boy of about eight entered, followed by a woman whose forehead was wrinkled with worry. The boy's hand was wrapped in a dish towel.

Drake stood. "What's the problem, Stavn?"

The woman spoke. "Stavn cut his hand trying to open a package with a knife." She glared at the boy. "He knew better. I'm afraid it's large enough to need stitches."

"I was trying to open the package without using my teeth." The boy sounded near tears.

Trice went down on her knees to eye level with the child. "Sometimes those things happen. I'm Dr. Shell. I'm going to be taking Dr. Stevansson's place. It's nice to meet you, Stavn. Do you mind if I have a look? I promise not to make it hurt."

Stavn hesitated, then slowly offered his hand.

Trice unwrapped the rag gently while holding pressure to his artery at his wrist, stopping the flow of blood. "Yep. That's a pretty deep and long cut. You must have been pushing really hard on the knife."

Stavn nodded, tears glistening in his eyes.

"Then I guess we better get you into an examination room and stitch that up." Drake directed Stavn and his mother down the hall. "Take the first room."

Trice accepted the hand Drake offered her. He pulled her to standing with seemly little effort.

"One of us better go make some pretty stitches." Trice grinned.

He left her to follow their patient. "I'll get the supplies while you settle Stavn."

Trice entered the examination room. "Stavn." Trice pulled a couple of plastic gloves from a box on the counter and tugged them on. She then rolled a small stool over beside the boy, who sat on the gurney. "May I see your hand again?"

The boy was quicker to let her see it than the last time.

She turned his hand over, palm side up. "Dr. Stevansson and I are going to clean it, then stitch it closed. Do you know what I mean by stitching?"

He nodded. "Yeah. Like my mother sews up my pants when I tear a hole in them."

"That's exactly right. We'll make it so it'll doesn't hurt. If it does, all you have to do is tell us, and we'll give you more medicine. There is one more thing you should know. We will have to give your hand a shot, so that might hurt for a sec. Then it'll be gone. You can hold your mother's hand, and it'll go by real fast."

Drake entered the room with a handful of supplies, making the space even smaller. He had a way of doing that. He looked at her. "You stitch and I'll bandage."

Was he testing her? "Sure." Her attention went to Stavn. "Is that okay with you?"

The boy agreed.

She took Stavn's hand once again. "I need a pan and saline."

Drake handed her the bottle. He held the pan under Stavn's hand.

She opened the bottle top. "We're going to pour this liquid over your hand. We have to wash it out really good."

Stavn sat still and rod straight as they worked.

Done, Trice picked up a towel and patted the area around the wound dry while Drake set the pan aside.

"All right, let's see what we've got here." Drake pulled back the cover of the suture kit. "Stavn, if you start to feel sick in your stomach, please tell us."

His mother said, "He has a pretty strong stomach."

"Famous last words," Trice mumbled. "All right, Stavn, I need you to lie on the table. Your mom can keep holding your hand, but she should move to the head of the bed." Thank goodness the mother followed her advice.

Trice helped Stavn lie on the table. "I want you to look at your mother. I have to give you that shot we talked about. It will only hurt for a second. It's important you be really still. After that, you can watch if you wish. If not, then look at your mom."

Drake handed her the syringe with the local anesthetic.

"Okay, here we go. Stavn, tell me what you like to do." She inserted the needle. "Do you like to ride a bicycle?"

The boy grunted a positive sound.

"I do too. I like to ride a mountain bike. I was sad when I couldn't bring one with me on the plane."

"I have a mountain bike too." The boy perked up.

Trice finished deadening the area. She touched around the spot. "Can you feel this?"

"No." The boy sounded unsure.

"Good. You are being so good. Dr. Stevansson, what kind of thread would you go with for a boy as strong as Stavn?"

Drake acted as if he were giving the question a great deal of thought. "I would select the heavier thread. He needs to have it really strong."

Thankfully Drake caught on to what she was doing. Putting the child at ease. "I agree."

Stavn glanced at his hand, then back at his mother.

Trice went to work stitching first the inside of the wound and then the outside. "Almost done." Two stitches later, she rolled back from the table. "You can look now."

The boy lifted his hand for a second, then put it down again.

Drake stepped forward. "Why don't you sit up while I bandage that for you?"

Stavn moved to the edge of the table.

Drake removed gauze from a package and made quick work of wrapping it around the boy's hand. He then secured it with plastic-covered tape. "This should keep it dry. I don't want you getting this hand wet. Ask for help when you need it. I would like to see you back tomorrow for a check." Drake looked at her. "Don't you think a day out of school is deserved?"

"I do." Trice smiled at Stavn.

The mother said, "Thank you. Both of you."

"You are welcome, Mary. I'm sorry. In all the excitement, I failed to introduce you to the new doctor. This is Beatrice Shell. Mary Leesdottir."

"Nice to meet you. Please call me Trice. Sorry we had to meet under these circumstances." Trice placed her hand on the boy's shoulder. "You have a brave son. Maybe show him where the scissors are so he can use them to open a package next time."

The mother smiled and nodded as she ushered Stavn out the door.

Drake turned to Trice. "I'm feeling good about leaving the clinic in your hands. You were excellent just now. You put Stavn at ease, and I've not seen better stitching." His grin grew. "Except maybe mine."

"Thank you for the seal of approval." She had to admit she liked having it.

Two evenings later, Drake rested in his recliner, half watching TV and half reading a book. Yet his thoughts were of Trice. She had been amazing with patients young and old over the last few days.

Stavn's injury hadn't been that extensive, but after Trice's help, Drake had complete confidence she would know how to handle whatever came her way. He shouldn't be spending time worrying about the clinic since he was the one who had chosen to leave. Trice had clearly made that point. To his great irritation.

The people in Seydisfjordur were no longer his responsibility. Despite his desire not to feel any responsibility, he did. That's what caused him to agree to step in when Dr. Johannsson passed away. Drake had had no intention of being here this long. He had been on his way to becoming a great surgeon. All his colleagues had said so. He'd done his part to help his home village, but now it was time to go.

With his parents having moved across the island, and his brother and sister there as well, there was no need to remain here. Drake only anticipated returning for short visits to see Luce, but he hoped one day soon she would agree to live with his parents. He could possibly return after completing his training, but that wasn't guaranteed despite the need for a surgeon in Seydisfjordur.

He had learned that quickly. While at university, he had enjoyed much of what a larger city offered. Returning to Seydisfjordur had been more difficult than he anticipated. Finding a wife, having a family were more problematic in the remote area. And even if he did find a wife in the city and wanted to move back, she might not agree.

He'd learned that the hard way when he brought a woman he was serious about home. At the time he had been considering returning. Dr. Johannsson had been encouraging him to take over the practice. His girlfriend hadn't enjoyed the flight, didn't like that there were no serious shopping places, and hated the outdoors. That was all before she saw the area in the dead of winter. Their relationship soon ended with her red-faced, snarled remark: "Nothing would entice me to ever live here!"

The subtext was, she didn't love him enough to consider it. That mistake he had no intention of repeating. He would take no chances. In London he could be a part of a practice, find a wife and settle down and be able to do surgery. He wanted to fulfill his dream, honor his grandfather, yet Seydisfjordur still pulled at him.

When the town needed the medical care he could provide, he had put his life on hold for them. Now that Trice was there, it was time for him to return to his training. Something that would give him a chance to help a larger number of people. Still, guilt ate at him when he thought of leaving.

He couldn't have it both ways. The discussion had been made. He would leave in little more than a week.

The next morning at the clinic, he called, "Trice, come up front when you're finished. I'll show you how to access charts on the computer. I also need to take you out back and show you how to handle the generator. It can be temperamental."

"Be right there." A few minutes later she approached the desk.

He stood and started toward the door. "We need to go outside to the back of the building."

She joined him.

They exited into the bright mid-day sunlight. The sight of the fjord and the mountain surrounding him always grabbed his attention. To Trice he said, "Tell me how you are planning to go about this research you have in mind."

"Is there a problem with me doing so?" Her tone had an edge to it as she stepped over the uneven ground.

"No, I was just curious."

"I'm particularly interested in the long-term effects HEP has on people. Studies have been done, but I believe there is more to learn. While I am here, it's the perfect opportunity to do research and write a paper. I would like to start by looking at files and then interviewing people."

He stepped up beside her and took the lead. "Files shouldn't be a problem. People might be more of one. I could help with that. Pave the way a little. Maybe I can get them to open up to you some. I know a few people who have had HEP and a couple of children. I'll need to speak to them before I share their names with you."

Her eyes brightened. "I understand. I appreciate any help you can give me before you go."

He stopped in front of the generator. "Come to think of it, there's a community event tonight. It would be a good way to meet people, to get to know them before you start asking them questions. If they interact with you some socially, then they'll be more likely to share."

Her look met his. "Is that how you are too?"

"I can be. Is there something you want to know?" He had the feeling she saw more of him than he wished.

She eyes narrowed when she angled her head to the side in thought. "I'm good for right now, but maybe I'll have something later."

"Okay. I'll honor that." Enough about him. They needed to get back to what they were doing here. "About the generator."

Fifteen minutes later after he'd explained the work of the machinery they head inside. "About tonight. Do you want to go?"

Trice smiled as if pleased with the idea She pushed the door open. "Of course. This will be my home for at least a year."

"If not more." She could get stuck here just as he had. Another doctor might not agree to take her place.

"Like you did?"

"Yes. If you are called to medicine, it is hard

to pull away when you are needed." *Especially when you know the people. When it is home.*

Trice met his look. "You're doing it."

He followed her inside. There was a note of accusation in her voice. He didn't like it. "I am, but I put my surgery career on hold for two years."

She looked over her shoulder. "Why is doing surgery day in and day out so important? You already have the skills. A practice. I bet you have gotten to use your skills here."

His jaw ticked like it had earlier. Who did she think she was, questioning his decisions? "I have, but mostly I've done general medicine stuff. Earaches, gout, and stitches, as you know. If I finish my fellowship, I can return to Reykjavík if there is a position in the hospital. Most of my family is on that side of the island now. Except for Luce. At least it is less than an hour away. I need to go if I'm going to, because they aren't going to hold my spot in London forever."

"Then I guess you have to go."

"You make that sound like a bad thing."

She shook her head. "It isn't bad. I just think you don't know your value here. But I shouldn't be convincing you to stay." She huffed. "If you did, I would lose my job."

He closed the door with a thud.

"So, are we on for the community center tonight?" Drake hoped she said yes. For some reason, he wanted to escort her.

She turned to face him. "I understand communities here are big on the folk arts."

"We aren't so much this time of the year. Tonight is a special occasion, but in the winter months, when it stays dark for so long and snow is falling and the cruise ships don't come, it's our opportunity for some culture and just getting together."

"Sounds like fun." Trice smiled.

"I'll pick you and Luce up at seven then."

"We could just meet you there."

He shook his head. "Not on your life. Luce would have my hide if I didn't escort you both."

"I wouldn't want to be the cause of that. I wasn't planning on working tonight, so I'd best let you walk us over." Trice had a grin on her lips as she headed down the hall.

Drake chuckled.


Trice turned the corner of Luce's house just as Drake did.

"Oof."

Strong hands cupped her upper arms, holding her in place. "Sorry to almost bowl you over. I was afraid I was running late."

Her heart jumped just being close to Drake. Why did he appeal to her so? It couldn't possibly be the fact he was good-looking, strong, intelligent and likable.

"Good evening," he said in a low, sexy drawl. "Are you ready for this?"

She backed away, smiling. "I'm not only ready. I'm looking forward to it."

"You're a brave woman. That Nordic blood in you is coming out."

Trice searched his face. "Are you talking about the town scaring me off?"

His face turned serious. "Maybe it should."

What did he mean by that?

He stepped back. "You look nice."

She couldn't help but blush. Her effort to impress him hadn't failed. The dress she had picked out was a lime color and went almost to her ankles. A tie of the same color encircled her waist. Dress boots in tan covered her feet.

"Different boots, I see."

She put out her foot and turned it one way, then another. "These are broken in."

"Good to hear." He pursed his lips and nodded.

"I'll have you know I'm wearing my other ones every night to break them in too." She threw her shoulders back proudly. "With heavy socks."

"I'm surprised you even put them back on your feet."

She met his gaze. "I'm not easily defeated."

"I'm learning that." Drake looked rather pleased with her statement.

"I want to get them wearable so I can explore

some more. I haven't really had a chance to do much of that. A good hiking trip would be fun."

"You should take some time while I am still here. You have been staying close to the clinic. We have been pretty busy, but I think most of the people who have come by the last couple of days weren't as sick as they were interested in meeting you."

Trice met Drake's look. He had such beautiful eyes. "It was nice to meet them. I hope to meet more tonight."

"Are you two going to the meeting or standing there all evening?" Luce's gravelly voice said from behind Drake.

Trice and Drake stepped back from each other.

Drake spoke first. "We were just on our way to get you."

The older woman harrumphed. She stood there with her purse on her arm, a little hat on her head and a shawl across her shoulders.

"You look lovely, Luce." Drake kissed her cheek.

"Don't you start trying to flatter me, boy," the older woman said, but she grinned.

He put his hands over his heart. "I wasn't trying to flatter you, Luce. I was telling you the truth."

"Let's go before all the good chairs are taken," the woman grumbled.

"Come on." Drake offered his arm to his

grandmother. "Let's get you to the community center."

A number of people entered the low block building ahead of them. They trailed behind them. Luce left them to join a friend. She and Drake found seats on a row about halfway up. Trice couldn't help but be excited about the coming program. This was a new adventure as far as she was concerned. She had a sense of being part of the community.

After all, she would be living here. This would be her world for the next year. She was already starting to fall in love with the place. It would be different in the winter months, but something deep down in her felt like it didn't matter what the weather was. She had found her place. This might be home. Was she jumping on the idea too soon?

She glanced at Drake. Or could it be someone who made her feel that way?

Trice enjoyed working with him. He was methodical and thorough, doing his job with a smile on his face, which indicated he loved his profession. She could see Drake's skills as he took care of his patients. He had capable hands. Drake would make an excellent surgeon.

But she would miss him. She suspected the entire town would. Those weren't emotions she should be having or encouraging.

# CHAPTER THREE

TRICE SAT STRAIGHTER at the sound of the guitar tuning. A group of people had settled on the stage. They looked as if they might be a family. The children were around the ages of ten and twelve. Everyone clapped, then quieted.

Trice shifted in her seat and clasped her hands in her lap. She must calm her nerves. Her hands trembled slightly. Oddly she felt a part of these people, included. Something that had rarely happened while she was growing up. She'd been lucky if she had spent over a year with a family until she was fifteen. Even with her last family, she had always been an outsider.

Drake leaned toward her. "Everything all right?"

She nodded. "Everything is wonderful."

He studied her a moment, then smiled.

She needed to appear confident in front of him. His support would be needed to get the village behind her.

"Hey." Drake placed a hand over hers for a moment.

"Yeah?"

"You'll be fine tonight."

For the next hour, they listened to the group play. The notes they could coax from their instruments were amazing. Their fingers would fly over the strings at times. Trice sat enthralled. More than once, she found herself tapping a toe.

When the concert was over, the crowd stayed for a potluck dinner.

Drake stood. "Let's have something to eat before they push back the chairs and tables to dance."

Dance. She hadn't expected that. Trice didn't consider herself a dancer.

They filled their plates with food stationed on two long tables.

"I didn't bring anything." Trice didn't want to look to the town as if she wasn't the type to do her share.

"Don't worry about it this time," a woman behind them said. "We will expect you to bring food next time. By the way, I'm Birta Atlasson. I heard how good you were with Stavn. I'm his aunt."

Trice said with true pleasure, "It's nice to meet you."

The line moved, and the woman's attention was caught by someone else.

Trice and Drake returned to where they had been sitting to eat. He went to get them drinks.

Returning, Drake handed her a cup. "Did you enjoy the music?"

"I did. I've never really done anything like this before. I'm enjoying it." She was too aware of him sitting close to her. The amount of attention Drake gave her both thrilled and disturbed her. Did the others notice? Maybe he was just being nice because she was new to town?

With everyone finished with their meal, the tables were pushed to the walls. Chairs circled the room. The family who played earlier returned to the stage. The rest of the crowd was invited to dance.

Trice touched Drake's arm. "I see Stavn and his mother over there." She indicated across the room. "I'm going to check on how his hand is doing."

Drake nodded and turned to speak to a man who had walked up.

Trice crossed the room, smiling at people as she went. Many returned her smile, but no one stepped out to introduce themselves. "Hey, Stavn. How's your hand today?"

He grinned when he saw her. "Look, I can move it now."

She went down on one knee, making sure her dress was tucked in at the right places. "Yes, you can. Don't get too sure of yourself until those stitches come out."

Trice stood and faced Stavn's mother. "Hi."

"Hi, Dr. Shell."

"Remember, it's Trice."

"Yes, that's right. Trice, I would like you to meet my friends." She introduced the three ladies standing nearby.

Trice had no hope of remembering their names, but she nodded and smiled. She would learn them all one day. She had been nervous earlier, but that had settled down. After a short conversation with the women, she looked over her shoulder to see Drake dancing with a young, slim, dark-haired woman almost his height. They were laughing as they moved.

"It didn't take Marie long to get Drake to dance with her," one of the women said.

"Nope. She will miss him when he's gone," said another.

"I hope he makes it out of town without her following him," the other commented.

Trice chest tightened. Her look stayed with the couple. Why did the women's words bother her? There wasn't anything going on between her and Drake. Trice had no right to feel concern. Yet she still wanted to know if Drake was involved with the pretty woman.

At the end of the song, Drake stepped away from the woman and headed toward their group. "Ladies, do you mind if I have a dance with Trice?"

"You might want to ask her," Stavn's mom snapped.

Drake's brows rose. "You are correct. Trice, would you care to dance?"

Trice took a step back. "I'm sorry. I don't really dance."

Stavn's mom's hand on her back stopped her movement and gave her a nudge. "Go on. You'll be fine. Drake will show you what to do."

Drake offered his hand. A new tune started, and the floor began to fill up. "Join me."

Still she hesitated. Stavn's mother nudged her again before Trice placed her hand in his. "You better take care of me."

Drake looked her in the eyes. His hand squeezed hers. "I will."

Something about the statement went straight to her heart. She could fall hard for his man who was going a different direction from her. She shouldn't let that happen. No scenario made that look like a good idea. But wouldn't it be okay to act on her daydreams, just for a little while?

Drake placed his arms around her but held her at a distance. "This is an Icelandic folk song. Follow my steps."

She put a foot out when he did. He turned her and she followed. There were awkward steps, but they continued around the floor.

"You are a natural." Drake grinned at her.

"Thanks. I don't feel like one." She worked to follow his movements.

"You'll catch on after you do it a few more times." He turned her and brought her to him.

"I hope so." She missed a step and caught up.

"There will be plenty of men to show you while you are here." His words were flat as he made a move.

Trice wasn't sure she liked that idea any more than the look on his face implied he did.

When the song ended, they went right into a slow song. Drake pulled her closer. She could feel his heat. Her hand lay lightly on his shoulder and was held securely in one of his hands. His other hand lay at her waist. It almost spanned the expanse of it. They swayed to the music.

"You looked pretty popular over there talking to Stavn's mother. Here I was thinking you were nervous about being in Iceland. You have been busy winning friends and influencing people."

"Stavn's mom was kind enough to introduce me around. That was nice of her."

"Did you ask about them knowing anyone with HEP?" He led her to the right.

"No, I figured I'd wait until they got to know me better."

He gave her waist a gentle squeeze. "Smart move. I think you'll do just fine here."

"I already know I like it here." She leaned

closer. "That woman you were dancing with is glaring at us."

He started to turn his head.

"No, don't look," she hissed. "I don't want her to know we're talking about her."

"It's just Marie. She's one of the nurses who comes in to help." His tone was dismissive.

She didn't look like she liked Trice much. "I'm going to have to work with her. By the look on her face, I don't think that will be much fun."

Drake shook his head. "You're being silly."

"You aren't the one she's glaring at."

Drake spun her. "You're right. She doesn't look happy."

"I think I'd better go. I don't need any drama in my days or nights. I don't need to step where I shouldn't since I'm new to town."

His grip tightened. "We've gone out a few times, but I have no claim on her or her on me."

"That's an interesting, old-fashioned way of putting things." Trice was trying to make a good impression, not become part of a soap opera.

"But it's true." Drake sounded anxious to have her believe him.

"Still, there's nothing between you and me, and I don't want her thinking there is. I better leave."

He let her hand go, and they walked off the floor.

Marie glided up to them. "Drake, aren't you going to introduce me to the new doctor?"

"Sure. Trice, I would like you to meet Marie Laxness. She will be helping you on clinic days."

Trice offered her hand. The woman took it after a moment of hesitation. "It's nice to meet you," Trice said.

Marie offered Trice a smile that didn't reach her eyes. "You too. I look forward to working with you."

Luce walked up with shawl in place, hat on her head and purse in hand. "Time to go."

"I'll get our coats." Drake left.

"Marie, how are you?" the older woman asked.

"Fine." Marie appeared unsure about Luce singling her out.

Luce's eyes narrowed. "Aren't you here a little early for a clinic next week?"

The other woman looked uncomfortable. "I came early to spend a long weekend with a friend"

"Mmm." There was no doubt from Luce's response she didn't believe that.

Drake returned, handing Trice her jacket. He pulled his on while she donned hers.Soon, she, Luce and Drake were outside in the cool air. They made their way home in silence.

At Luce's door, Trice said, "Good night."

"Give me a sec with Luce, and then I'll walk you to your door."

"That's not necessary." Trice continued on. As

she turned the corner, she heard Luce say, "Don't you hurt that girl, boy. You're leaving here."

It had only been daylight two hours when Drake knocked on Trice's door. No sound. She must sleep like the dead. This time he banged on the door loud enough that he was afraid he might wake Luce. If Trice didn't answer soon, he would have to leave her. Relief washed through him at the rattle of the door handle.

Trice opened the door a crack. "Drake, what's wrong?"

"We've got an emergency. Get dressed and bring those boots you've been breaking in. You will need them. Also, the heaviest jacket you have. You got five minutes while I get supplies from at the clinic."

"I'll be ready in four." She slammed the door.

He shook his head in amazement. Trice was tough as nails. He rarely drove his truck, but he didn't have time to walk the distance to the air-port. Trice hurried up as he came out of the clinic. She had a black bag with a red cross on the side in her hands.

"Let me have that." He reached for her bag. "Hop in." She did as he requested, and he placed their bags in the back of the truck.

"What happened?"

"There was an accident at Fjaroara Falls. A hiker slipped and fell. Rescue was called. As the rescuer and the hiker were being pulled up, there was a rockfall. They are both injured now. One hanging and unconscious. The other stuck on a small ledge. We are the medical care who could get there the fastest." He pulled into the airport.

"What're we doing here?" Trice tried to keep her voice even.

"We're flying there. That's why we can get there so fast." He hopped out of the truck, going around to retrieve their bags.

Trice climbed out slower.

Drake was halfway to the plane before he realized she wasn't with him. He turned to find her still beside the truck, staring at the plane. "Is something wrong?"

"I don't really do planes, and not small ones." Her voice was so low he had to strain to hear her.

He didn't have time for this. "If you are going, then you'll have to this time."

She looked around. "Where is the pilot?"

"Right here." He touched his chest.

Her voice rose an octave. "You have a pilot license?"

"I do." He started for the plane once more.

She hustled after him. "You really know what you're doing?"

He opened a storage door on the side of the aircraft and placed their bags inside, then closed the compartment. "Yes, I know what I'm doing. You better get in. I'll take care of you."

When she didn't move right away, he said, "Well?"

"I'll go," she announced, sounding braver than she felt.

Drake opened the passenger door and helped her up on the wing so she could climb in. The woman was featherlight but had a will of iron. "Get in and buckle up. I'll close the door for you."

He did so. On his way to the other side, he checked the plane and soon settled in his seat. Minutes after going through the checklist, he had them rolling down the runway.

Trice hadn't said a word or moved the entire time. He'd not had a chance to reassure her, and he felt the tension rising off her in the cockpit. They were in the air and flying steady when he glanced at her. "You know if you open your eyes, you can see this beautiful morning. You don't want to miss this view."

"If I do open my eyes, I'll also see us crash."

He chuckled. "You don't have much faith in me, do you?"

"I didn't mean for it to sound like that." She still had her eyes closed tight, and her hands clutched the edge of her seat.

"I know."

"But I'm scared."

He grinned. "That's obvious. How about trying to open one eye?"

"Oh, my." Her soft sigh a few seconds later had

him thinking he would like to do something to her that would elicit that reaction.

"It gets me every time too. Keep your focus eye-level. Don't look down. But look at this land. It's beautiful."

"It is lovely. I don't see how you can leave it." As she became caught up in their conversation, she had eased her fingers off the console and re-laxed in the seat.

"You would if you had planned and worked toward being a surgeon most of your life. If you wanted to live where people like Luce didn't have an opinion about what you do. If you would like to buy something and not wait a month for it to come."

"I would love to have people who cared like that about me."

He glanced at her. The vulnerability on her face pulled at his heart. What he had, she wanted. She had a way of making him see what he would be missing when he left. "I can understand that, but it can get to be a bit much sometimes. Often."

"It's hard for me to even imagine that. Grow-ing up as a foster kid, I never had anyone who really cared enough to offer much advice." A few minutes of silence passed before she asked, "How long have you been flying?"

"Most of my life. My father is a pilot. I learned from him but also took flying lessons. Somebody in town needs to know how to fly. I wanted to learn."

She looked around the cockpit. "Does the plane belong to you?"

"It does." He was proud of the airplane.

Trice relaxed some in her seat. "What will you do with it when you leave?"

"I'll fly to Reykjavík. John, the pilot who brought you in, will bring it back when he can."

"But doesn't it need somebody to fly it once in a while?" Her attention stayed on the view ahead.

"John will use it when he needs it. When you need him to fly somewhere, he'll take you."

"Not in my game plan to do this too often. If you weren't staying and I didn't come here, what would happen with the medical service up here?"

"A traveling doctor would come once a week. There's always somebody in a community who rises to be the go-to person for medical care. Or a nurse might even be persuaded to take the job. Just stay here full-time."

"Like Marie?"

He didn't miss the tight note in Trice's voice at Marie's name. Was she jealous despite him saying there was nothing between him and Marie? He liked the idea. It meant Trice might care. "Yes, like Marie. But she will not stay. She has already been asked." He dropped altitude.

Trice grabbed the seat. "Why're we going down?"

"Because we're almost there." He went to work landing them.

"That didn't take long."

"It never does if you fly, but it would've been a long walk and a longer drive. The roads between here and Seydisfjordur are not that well cared for. There's a short airstrip here. It's the only reason I was called. They knew I could get here."

"I won't be much help in cases like this if I'm not able to fly."

"This trip is an anomaly. You won't be called on for something this far away." He pushed and pulled a few knobs. Then adjusted the flaps.

Soon they were scooting along the runway to a stop. Drake looked at Trice. "I'm proud of you. At least you kept your eyes open."

She glared at him. "You should've been watching what you were doing instead of me."

"You were much more entertaining, and I could land the plane with my eyes closed."

"I'm glad you didn't." She unbuckled. "This was a good lesson. I'm learning to focus on things like the morning sunrise or what I want to do bad enough to try something that scares me."

"You have a point there."

Before he had turned the engines off, a truck had pulled up nearby. Drake climbed out of the plane and went around to help Trice down. She'd managed to open and close the door. Their bags were sitting on the wing. Apparently, she was determined she would be of help and not a hindrance. He liked that.

He offered his hand, and she jumped down to stand beside him.

"Stevansson?" asked the truck driver.

"Yep. And this is Dr. Shell."

"They're waiting on you up at the falls." The man pointed up the valley.

"We're ready when you are." Drake threw the bags in the back seat of the heavy-duty truck. Trice took a seat beside them, and he climbed in the front.

"Tell us what's going on. All the information I got was I was needed for backup. That a rescuer was injured along with a hiker."

"The hiker stepped over the rail before daylight, as they do when they want to get the just-right sunrise picture, and hit a slick spot and went down. Thankful he hit a ledge. Rescue was called. They went after him. On his way down, his large body caused a rockfall. Now there are two injured men. One with a head injury and the other with a broken leg. We need to get them both up. Let you do what you can before we get them out of here. A storm is coming in, and we're not sure a helicopter will make it in time. Your accessibility to a plane was why we called you. There was no time to wait. We've got to get these men out."

Relief washed through Trice as her feet settled back on the ground. When Drake had driven up to the plane, she'd thought her body would refuse to get in it. She had barely made it flying into Seydisfjordur. But she had to go. She and Drake had people needing their help waiting on them. If this was the best way to get there, then she'd have to make it work. It would have been nice if she could have kept her fear from Drake, but he'd seen it right away. He'd left her no choice but to admit to it.

He had managed to coax her to open her eyes and control her breathing.

After she had gotten over her initial fear of flying and being in such a small plane, she'd started to enjoy it. It had been reassuring being in Drake's hands. It calmed her nerves enough to at least enjoy part of the view. The beauty of the countryside in the early morning took her breath away.

This was a lifestyle she would have to get used to during the year ahead. She had wanted to come to Iceland, to find herself and her heritage. She couldn't close her eyes to that or her job responsibilities. She had to step up and do what must be done.

Now they were barreling down a narrow paved road. Ten minutes later, the man driving came to a neck-jerking stop and hopped out. She and Drake followed after grabbing their bags. He took hers from her as they started toward the group standing near the edge of the falls. Water rushed nearby with a deafening roar, creating a mist that filled the air and blew toward them.

Trice shivered. This wouldn't be much fun. But staying warm and dry would be a problem for later. Right now, the injured men were the worry.

The driver joined the group of other official-looking people. The circle opened when she and Drake approached.

Now it was time for a serious discussion. The hiker and the EMT had already been in the ravine for hours. Not only the injuries but the elements were working against them. Daylight helped, but the dark clouds gathering would not. They must be brought to safety right away.

"I'm Dr. Stevansson, and this is Dr. Shell. What can we do to help?" Drake asked.

"Glad to have you here." The man looked at her. "Both of you. We have one with a head injury hanging nine meters down, dangling from a line, and another with a possible broken leg. The rescuer, the best we can tell, is unconscious, and the one with the broken leg is another eight meters below him on a ledge. He has little mobility. We have to get some medical help down there, but the space is small. We need no more rockfalls. The conditions are wet and slippery. We're trying to work out the logistics now."

Trice said without thinking, "I'll go."

# CHAPTER FOUR

DRAKE COULDN'T BELIEVE what he'd just heard. He along with the group turned and looked at her.

"Trice, I can't let you do that."

"It's not for you to say. I have some rock-climbing experience. I have the medical knowledge, and I am the smallest person here. I have to go."

Drake could do nothing but glare at her with his heart in his throat.

"Are you sure about this?" one of the men asked.

Trice squared her shoulders. "No, but I don't think there's a choice. I can do some quick triage easement and treatment if necessary, and then you can bring them up."

One of the rescue men, after crossing his arms on his chest, said, "I do appreciate your offer, but I don't think you are qualified, and we certainly don't need a third party down there making matters worse."

Drake watched in bemusement as Trice crossed her arms over her chest, too, and glared at the man. "And if you had a better plan, I think you would be executing it by now."

The man closed his mouth with surprise as if dumbfounded. He blinked.

Drake decided to intervene. "She has a point. We need to get these men up and to help before this storm rolls in."

The man shook his head. "Okay. I don't know that I have a choice. I'll get the harness."

Drake turned his back to the others and pulled her around to face him. "Are you absolutely sure? You've only been in Iceland for a week."

"I'm sure. If I don't do it, who will?" She met his look.

Drake didn't have an answer.

"I know rock climbing. I'm not afraid of heights, and I certainly know medicine. More importantly, I'm the smallest and lightest person here. That makes me the most qualified."

She had a point, but he didn't like it. "But you don't like flying."

"That's different. But we can argue about that later. Don't we want to get these people out of there safely and with as little additional injury as possible?"

Drake shook his head. "I still don't like the plan."

The mountain rescuer returned with harness and rope in hand.

"You don't have to like it to go along with it."
She turned to the man.

As the rescuer rigged her up, Trice said to
Drake, "Talk this through with me."

That statement told him Trice didn't feel as
much bravado as she tried to show.

She didn't wait on him to begin. Her look im-
plored him. A flash of fear went through her eyes.
"Explain exactly what I need to do. I can perform the medical assessment with no problem,
but what else should I look for? If those guys have
been down there for hours, they'll need blankets,
even heat packets to put inside their jackets to
warm their cores."

"Are you finished?" Drake asked the rescuer
doing her harness.

He nodded.

"Give us a minute, please?"

The man walked away.

Drake's hands went to her shoulders, and his
look met hers. "You've got this. You'll be lowered slowly. Keep your feet and hands against the
rock. I'll make sure you have some gloves. You
will assess the injured rescuer, then see that he
gets up to the top safely. Then you'll have to go
back after the man with the broken leg."

"I'll need my bag."

"I will see that it is sent down to you. Along
with splints and supplies." He placed a small ear-
piece in her ear. "Through this, you can talk to

me the entire time Tell me what you need. You'll be able to hear me too. Now, how are you doing?"

"You will be there with me?"

"I'll never leave you." That wasn't exactly true. He would be leaving her in a few days. But for now, he was here for her.

Trice walked toward the edge of the cliff with Drake beside her.

She put out a hand, stopping him. "Don't go any closer. I don't want you to slip. You need to be tied off." She had been secured to a truck winch. The rope stretched across the ground.

"I don't like this plan at all." Drake's mouth went into a tight line.

"I'll have this over and done before you come up with another way, and you know it." She reassured him as well as herself.

His look bore into hers. "You be careful. I'll be right here waiting."

Trice stood in front of Drake as he switched on the light attached to her helmet. "You are going to need this."

"Step back a little bit," one of the rescuers called. "You're getting mighty close. We don't need to have another person down there."

Trice nudged him back. "He's right. It's slippery here. If people—" she gave him a pointed look with a forced grin "—would read the posted rules, then there would be no need for us to do this."

He returned her smile. "Point taken." He walked to a safe distance from the edge.

She looked at him. "Any other ideas or suggestions?"

"Other than I wish it was me going?"

Was he really that worried about her? "I'll be as quick as I can. I promise."

All her worries and fears went out of her head when he approached again, cupped her cheek and gave her a long look. For a moment, it crossed her mind he might kiss her. Then he said, "Be careful."

She blinked. "I will be."

Two of the rescue team who were tied off joined them. She gave Drake a last look and walked to the edge with the men.

Trice leaned back, holding the rope between her legs with one hand behind her back and the upper part of the same rope with her other hand, bracing with her feet against the stone wall to rappel down the cliff. She glanced below at the boulders and water rushing over them. This was nothing like rock climbing in a gym. She swallowed hard.

Drake's voice came in her ear. "You got this. Slow and easy."

It was good to hear his voice. He had a nice one. She let out the breath she had been holding. "Okay."

"How far away are you from the first man?"

"You can hear me?"

"Yes. The radio has an automatic mic."

"Oh, okay. He is about twelve feet from me… uh… I mean four meters from me now. He's just hanging there. I see no movement."

"Trice, where did you learn to rock climb?"

She moved slowly down. "In the gym of the university. I did it for exercise. Who would have thought it would have paid off like this?"

"You keep surprising me."

A few minutes later, she said, "I've reached him. He's unconscious." She hung there, balancing herself to stay upright. Then she looked down. The man with a broken leg was on the other side of the crevice. "Hey, can you hear me?"

"I hear you, Trice."

"Sorry. I'm calling to the man with the bad leg."

A man below her groaned. Then she heard a weak, "Yes."

"I'm here to help. Stay put. I have to get this man out of the way before I can come after you. But I promise I am coming."

"Hurry," came the man's low response.

"I'll be there as soon as I can." She couldn't afford to hurry. Haste could create mistakes. She fought to turn the man so she could see his face. "Drake, I'm doing the assessment on the first man now."

She pulled the digital thermometer from where

it hung on her vest. Running it over the man's forehead, she read the numbers. "He has a low-grade fever. Pulse eighty over sixty. Breathing slow but pathway clear."

Wrapping her legs around the man's knees and locking her heels, she held him close enough that she could lift one eyelid. She shined her light in his face. "Pupils are fixed and dilated."

"Roger that," Drake's voice came back.

"He has a crack in his helmet, but it's still secure to his head. He took a good hit. He's too heavy for me to do much with. Tell the guys to start pulling him up. I'm coming too to guide him between the rocks. I need to stay between him and the sides so he doesn't have further injury."

"But Trice—"

"Drake, there isn't time to argue. Just don't let our ropes get tangled, and pull them at the same speed." Trice turned so her back was to the rock face. She held the man with her legs and arms. "Go slow."

With a tiny jerk, she started moving up. The man moved as well. When she could, she used a hand to push off the wall in an effort to protect her back. She misjudged an outcropping and took a long drag over a sharp rock.

"Ouch."

"Trice?" Drake's panic-stricken voice came over the radio.

"I'm fine. Let's get this man up." She couldn't worry about her back now.

"Take care of yourself first. You're no help to that guy or the other one if you get hurt. I see you. You're almost here. Slow and easy."

"You shouldn't be so close to the edge." She didn't need Drake falling.

"I'm tied off and lying on the ground. Okay, let go of the man. We can take him from here."

She released the man, and he was slowly lifted past her until he disappeared over the top.

Drake said, "I'm going to leave you to see about this man. I'll be back soon. One of the rescue people is going to be here with you."

Trice couldn't deny she hated to lose Drake's reassuring voice. She could get used to it. And she shouldn't.

"Hello, Dr. Shell. This is Sunna. I'll be with you until Dr. Stevansson can return. Are you going down again?"

"Please call me Trice. Send me down before I back out."

"Trice, your rope has been released to you. You are free to rappel," the woman's voice assured her.

Once again placing her hands in the correct position, Trice started down the wall again. "Please talk to me, Sunna. Are you from around here?"

"Born and raised. I understand you are from

America. Heck of an introduction to Iceland being part of this show."

Trice had made it to where the first man had been. "Mister, I'm coming," she called to the injured man. Her back screamed with pain, but she kept moving. "Sunna, I'm going to have to swing over to the edge in a moment."

"I'm glad you let me know. Dr. Stevansson threatened my life if I let anything happen to you."

Warmth washed through Trice. "Nothing is going to happen to me. Okay, here I go. My rope may go slack. I'll try to sit on the edge." Trice pushed off the wall and almost made the edge.

The man half lay and half sat, his legs stretched in front of him.

Trice spoke to Sunna. "I'm too high. I'm going down a few feet and trying again." This time she was successful. She managed to reach the ledge and sit on it near the man's feet. "Made it."

Trice went to work immediately, telling the man, "We're going to get you out of here as soon as possible. What's your name?"

"Mark Richards."

"I'm Trice. I'm a doctor. Tell me where you hurt." Trice did a visual assessment using her headlamp.

"My left leg. Just below the knee."

"I need to touch it. It may hurt." Trice gently probed the man's leg from above the knee down, until the man winced. "I feel the break. It'll need to be splinted before you can be moved. I want you to lie back and take deep breaths. Sunna, are you still there?"

"Right here."

"Please send down my med bag, a blanket and the splints. Dr. Stevansson should have gotten everything ready. Also send some drinking water. You will need to swing the rope if you can in order for me to reach it."

Sunna responded immediately. "I'll have it down in a moment."

Trice turned back to the man. "I need to get your vitals. Just lie still. This shouldn't take but a few minutes." She quickly went about getting his heart rate, respiration rate and temperature. "Other than a broken leg and being stuck down here, I would say you are a lucky man."

The man grunted, clearly not impressed with her appraisal.

Sunna's voice filled the air. "Trice, the supplies you requested are coming down."

Trice looked up. The light landed on the stuff hanging from the end of a rope. "I see it. Swing it."

She missed the first pass. On the second she managed to snatch the edge of the bag and bring it in. "Got it. Don't move."

The rope slackened. Trice quickly removed the rope and set the bag and splints between the man and the wall, making sure they wouldn't be lost to the rocks and water below.

"Mark, I'm going to splint your leg. Before I do that, I'm going to give you a pain pill, because you'll need it on the way up." She located the pill bottle in her bag and was pleased to find two bottles of water tucked in the bag as well.

She handed both to the man.

"Trice?" Sunna's voice.

"Yes?"

"Everything okay? Dr. Stevansson wants to know."

"All is well. I'm getting ready to put the splints on now." She wasn't used to this much concern from one person. It would be easy to get used to. Especially when it was from Drake.

After placing the splints on either side of Mark's leg, she began to secure them with a flexible bandage. Wrapping the leg until it would not move, she soon had Mark ready to transport.

"Sunna, what is the plan for bringing him up?"

"We're sending down a harness. You'll need to strap him in."

Trice packed the leftover supplies into her bag. "Send it down. I'll need instructions. I'm getting a little punchy, and my fingers are cold. I don't want to make a mistake."

"Harness is on the way down. I'll talk you through it."

A minute later, the harness was in Trice's hands. "I'm ready when you are."

"Here we go," Sunna said. "Hold the harness by the D-ring. Shake it out so all the straps fall. Unbuckle any buckles."

"Done."

"Put the shoulder straps on first," Sunna continued.

"Hold on a sec, Sunna." Trice spoke to Mark. "You'll need to sit up as much as you can." She helped Mark with the straps while making sure she didn't go off the edge. "Legs straps next. Right, Sunna?"

"Yes."

"Mark, this is where we're going to have to be careful. You'll need to lift yourself with your arms so I can reach under you for the straps. Tell me when you're ready."

The man lifted his back and hips. Trice ran her hands beneath him until she found the straps, pulling them out between his legs. He quickly lowered his hips with a loud sigh. Trice secured the lock on one leg and then the other.

"Trice?"

The sound of Drake's voice vibrated through her. "Hey. How's the other patient doing?"

"He should be fine with time. He's off in a helicopter." His voice dropped lower as if they were alone. "Are you all right?"

"I'm fine. Will you help me lift this man up? I'm ready to get out of here."

"I'll be glad to see you." There was a pause as if he might be collecting his emotions. "So, where are you with the harness?"

"I'm locking the breast strap now." Her cold fingers worked with the metal.

"Be sure to pull out any excess in the shoulder straps. They need to be snug." Drake's voice had turned anxious-sounding.

"Done."

"Good. The rope is coming down with the caliper. Clip it on the D-ring. Make sure it closes."

"You have to swing the rope for me to reach it." She caught it on the first arc. "Got it. Clipping it on now."

With the caliper firmly closed, she said, "We're ready down here. Tell them to go slow and easy."

"Will do."

"Mark, I'll be going up with you. Making sure you don't hit the wall. Help me by keeping yourself off the wall using your hands. I'll be between you and the rock."

Mark nodded.

Trice studied him a moment. He wouldn't be the help she hoped for. He'd been through as much as his body and mind could stand. "Mark, give me five more minutes before you pass out if you can."

He muttered something unintelligible.

She was losing him quickly. Scooting along the edge as far as she could, Trice used her hand to steady his leg as he was lifted into the air. "Hold him there. Now bring me up." She swung out to take the man by the arms, making sure she was between him and the rock face. "Okay, we're ready."

They move slowly up. She said nothing for a few minutes.

"Trice? Talk to me."

"We are fine. We'll be there in a minute." She winced as her back brushed the wall.

"You okay down there? That sounded like pain."

"All's good. Just ready to be on firm ground again." She checked her patient. He had passed out. All the while, she could hear Drake giving instructions on what would be needed for the incoming patient.

"I see you."

Trice looked up. She focused on Drake's handsome face. "Hold me here and bring Mark on up. He has passed out, so he won't be any help."

Mark moved above her and was pulled over the side.

She held the man's good leg so he wouldn't swing more than necessary. "Careful of that leg. I did the best I could in the cramped space."

"Looks good to me." Drake sounded impressed.

Seconds later she was lifted over the side and drawn to a safe place away from the cliff.

A woman stood in front of her. "Nice to meet you, Trice. I'm Sunna. Dr. Stevansson is with the patient. He told me in no uncertain terms to help you and see that you were taken care of."

"I don't think that's necessary. I'm fine." Trice's fingers fumbled with the lock on her harness.

"Let me help you with that." Sunna came to stand in front of her.

Trice flexed her fingers back and forth. "My fingers seem incapable of moving all of a sudden."

Sunna reached for the breast lock. "I'm sure they are cold. We'll get you over to the truck and warm you up."

Trice was amazed at how she had managed to go from doing research to rescue work. "I should check on the patient."

Sunna held the harness in one hand and took Trice's arm in the other. "Dr. Stevansson said you would say that, but he wants you checked out, and I am to take you to the truck. Please don't get me in trouble."

Drake's heart had thumped against his chest as Trice came over the side. He only had time to glance at her to make sure she was really there before his attention returned to their patient.

He hated that he couldn't go to her, but the man needed to be readied for travel.

He didn't know why he was so concerned about Trice. She wasn't anyone to him, yet the anxiety that ran through his veins screamed something different. His heart had only started to truly beat again when she had safely been pulled out of the falls.

He had instructed Sunna to care for Trice, but he was still anxious to check on her himself.

Moments later he heard her voice beside him. "What can I do to help?"

His head jerked up. "What are you doing here? I've got this." He looked beyond Trice to Sunna, who threw her hands in the air as if she had tried to stop Trice. "You did a good job down there. Go take care of yourself."

"But—"

"He's almost ready to go. I'll give you a full report in a few minutes. I don't need another patient today. Please do as I ask. If not for your sake, then mine."

Trice didn't look happy, but she joined Sunna, and they walked toward the truck he and Trice had arrived in.

Goodness, what had happened to make Trice so resilient? To think he had been worried about her being able to handle the conditions during the winter. She was more than up to it and anything else Iceland dished out. She certainly had more backbone than the other women he'd been interested in. Interested in? Yes, he was attracted to her.

He finished giving his report to the ambulance EMT. The injured man had a long, uncomfortable ride ahead of him. A big, fat raindrop landed square on top of Drake's head. It was time for them to get out of there. "He's all yours, fellows. Good luck on the drive down to the hospital. Be careful."

Drake waited until the man was loaded safely in the ambulance, then jogged to the truck just as it began to rain in earnest. A roll of thunder and a flash of lightning went across the sky as he reached for the back seat door handle.

As he climbed in beside Trice, Sunna climbed out the driver's seat. She had the truck running, and it was warm inside. "I need to go help wrap up and make a report."

"Thanks, Sunna. I owe you one." Drake climbed in beside Trice.

"Me too," Trice said.

Sunna smiled. "You are both welcome. See you around."

Trice sat with her arms across her chest, shaking.

"You need to get those wet clothes off." He shifted to look at her.

Trice glared. "Don't you get in and start giving orders. Especially when you're telling me to take off my clothes."

Drake couldn't help but grin. "There's my Trice."

Her fingers went to the zipper of her jacket but failed to bend enough to hold it. "I'm not your Trice."

Drake studied her a second. He wasn't sure that was true. "Let me help with that." He reached for the zipper pull and opened her coat, then helped her remove the wet material, dropping it on the floor.

Trice picked up a blanket from the seat.

Drake adjusted it around her shoulders. He was as damp from the mist, the rain and lying on the ground as she was, but he didn't acknowledge it. His concern remained on her.

The driver who had brought them to the site climbed in the driver's seat. "I'll see you get to some warmth and food. We really appreciate your help today." He drove along the road they had come on. "The rescue leader has already made arrangements for a room at a resort not far from here where you can warm up and rest."

Trice gave Drake a questioning look.

"There is no flying out of here today." Drake observed the pouring down rain.

Ten minutes later, the driver pulled into a gravel parking lot in front of a small cabin and handed Drake a key.

Drake climbed out and offered his hand to Trice to help her down. "I'll carry you in."

"No, you won't. I've got this."

"You don't even have shoes on." She had taken them off before he'd climbed in the truck. "It'll be much faster my way."

"No."

Drake gave up arguing. "Then I'll get your clothes and boots. Run for the porch."

She hurried away.

Drake grabbed their belongings, thanked the driver, and stalked up the steps to join Trice. "Get the door." He nudged her with a hand to her back. "We need to get in out of this."

Trice yelped.

His look searched her. "What's wrong? Are you hurt?"

"Just a scrape."

"Go inside. I need to have a look." Drake followed her, dropping her wet coat and boots in the floor along with their bags.

"Turn around and let me see your back." He reached for her.

She took a step out of reach. "I'm sure it will be fine. I'll shower and clean it well."

"Like you can take care of something on your back. I'm a professional. Let me judge." He came toward her.

"And I'm not?"

"Trice, I'm too tired and my nerves have been

stretched too far for you to be so difficult. Let me see. I can take care of it easier than you can. If you could reach it."

She was impossibly independent. "Let me get out of these wet clothes first. But I don't have anything else to put on."

He pulled a blanket off the back of the sofa and handed it to her. "Go to the bedroom and take them off, wrap up in this, lie on the bed and call me."

"Do you always make such demands on women?"

He looked at her and quirked his mouth. "You choose now to try to be funny." He took her by the shoulders and turned her in the direction of an open door. "I don't have to make demands to get a woman into bed. Now go do as I say. I'll get a fire started."

Trice disappeared into the bedroom. He went about finding a match to light the fire, which had already been laid. With that done, he removed his boots and stripped off as many clothes as possible while leaving enough to remain decent.

"Trice? Are you ready yet?"

"Yes."

Drake picked up his medical bag and headed for the bedroom. Trice lay on the bed on her stomach just as he had directed her to.

She shivered. "I don't know if I'll ever be warm again."

"You will," he assured her. "Promise. I'll try to be as fast as I can with this. Then you can get in a warm shower. Then come sit by the fire." He sat on the edge of the bed. "I'm going to bring the blanket down just low enough for me to see your injury."

She said nothing as he pulled the blanket away from her body and lowered it. He winced when he saw the angry bruised line down her back, thankful there were no abrasions or open wounds. At least her clothes had protected her some.

"When did this happen?"

"When I was bringing the first man up." Her voice was muffled against the bed.

"Oh, Trice. You should have said something. We could have figured out another way."

"There wasn't one. They were depending on me."

He knew that feeling well. Hadn't he been living that for the last two years? He pulled the blanket up, covering her to the neck, not allowing himself to step out of doctor mode no matter how much he might want to. "You don't have any broken skin. Which is good. I'll let you get a shower. Then I'll put some cream on it that Luce swears by. It has always helped my aches and pains."

Trice said nothing. The soft sound of even breathing was all he heard. She was asleep. Trice was exhausted after her heroic work. He couldn't blame her.

Drake pulled the corner of the bedcover over her, making sure her feet were tucked under. Unable to resist, he brushed her hair away from her face. "That Viking blood served you well."

# CHAPTER FIVE

TRICE ENTERED THE toasty warm living room. A fire blazed in the fireplace. She pulled the blanket tighter around her. Her clothes were hung on chairs circling the fire. Drake had been busy and thoughtful.

He wasn't there, but he lingered everywhere, especially in her thoughts. He had shown such tenderness before she'd gone down over the cliff. His voice had held concern when he had spoken to her, reassuring her he was there with her. Rarely had she had that in her life.

The bravado she had shown him had been forced. She had been terrified. Relief had swept through her, and adrenaline had washed her energy away after she reached the truck. She'd done what must be done and hoped it didn't happen again. She had lived much of her life that way. The exception was that this morning, it had affected others' lives. They had needed her assistance, or they might have died.

She fingered her clothes, but they were still

damp. Her boots lay on their sides with the mouths open as wide as possible. Drake had thought of everything. Taking a seat on the sofa, she brought her feet up under her. If she was this cold this time of year, how was she going to handle the winter?

A sound at the door drew her attention. Drake entered with a bag in his hand and kicked the door closed with his foot. "Well, hey. I hope you're hungry. I have some soup and sandwiches here."

"I am. Where did you get those?"

"I've been over to the main office and then to the restaurant. I have coffee going here, but would you rather have something else?"

"Hot tea would be nice."

He set the bag down on the table. "It just so happens there's some tea bags here as well, and one electric burner. I'll heat some water. How are you feeling?"

"Better now with sleep and a shower. Have you had either?" She turned to see him better.

"I took a shower. My morning wasn't as physically demanding as yours. You earned the rest." His eyes focused just below her face.

Trice glanced down. The blanket had slipped, showing a generous portion of her shoulder and the rise of one breast. She met his glaze and pulled the material back into place. The look of disappointment in his eyes satisfied in a way she hadn't expected.

He blinked, then turned to the electric eye. "I'll have this ready in a minute."

Drake acted as if he were a little uncomfortable. "Is there something I can do to help?"

"No, I've got it."

She stood and adjusted the blanket, tucking it in so it stayed in place, then pulled a throw off the sofa over her shoulders. She wasn't a fashion statement, but she was covered and warm.

"Take a seat at the table." Drake set out the food from the bag. His attention remained on his actions.

She joined him, taking one of the two wooden chairs at the small table. "Have you heard how our patients are doing?"

"The helicopter landed just before the storm broke. The man with the head injury is conscious but has a banging headache. He should completely recover. The one with the leg injury is still on his way. It takes four hours to get him to the nearest hospital, but at least he could go by ambulance."

"Sorry I fell asleep on you."

"Understandable. Your back thankfully isn't too bad. You will be sore more than anything. I need to put that cream on it before you go to bed tonight to help with the ache in the morning. How are you feeling now?"

"Like I've done all the climbing I want to for some time." She grinned.

He glanced up. "I would imagine. All of that was pretty intense."

"It was. Does the practice take part in stuff like that often?" She took the top off the bowl of soup.

"Today was more the exception than the rule."

"That's good to know. I'm not sure I could take it on if I thought it happened regularly."

Especially if he wasn't there to work with her.

"You certainly impressed the rescue squad. They couldn't praise you enough. I know of two men who were glad you were there."

"And you as well. I can't take much credit for my size, how my mom and dad created me." She hadn't thought of her mom and dad in a long time. Who they were. Where her father was. If he was alive or dead. Even what he looked like.

"Do you know anything about them?" he asked quietly.

"No. You know about my mother. I don't even have an idea who my father was or is." She didn't want to stay on this subject. "I'm hungry. Let's eat before the soup gets cold."

He took the chair across from her. Both started eating with gusto.

"This soup is really good. I was starving. I missed two meals today. One from when some crazy man woke me up before the birds to force me to fly around in an airplane, then stood around looking down as I went into a hole."

He grinned. "I might know that person."

"I thought you might." She enjoyed recovering in this cozy cabin with Drake, a flickering fire, and hot soup that filled her stomach and mellowed her mood. She liked being with him. Too much.

"We're socked in for a while. I found a few board games in the back if you want to play."

She looked at the window. Rain still came down. It only made matters worse, forcing them closer together.

"Will Seydisfjordur be okay without us?"

"I'm sure they are. You do know you won't have to be glued to the place. You can have a life too. Even be gone overnight."

She propped her elbows on the table and studied him. "What do you do with your free time?"

"I go hiking in the mountains. Even in a quiet place, you need to get away sometimes."

"Is that why you want to leave so badly?"

His eyes held a defiant look. "No, it's because I want to use my surgery skills. There isn't enough going on in Seydisfjordur for that to happen. If you haven't noticed, there is no operating theater attached to the clinic."

"Seems to me that based on today's activities, there is plenty to keep you busy. Maybe not with surgery, but certainly being needed."

"Being needed is important to you, isn't it?"

She shrugged. "It is better than no one knowing you are alive."

Drake averted his eyes. Had she really lived like that? He couldn't imagine not having someone who really cared. Seeing what it meant to her made him appreciate it more.

He had actually noticed how much he was needed. For the first time in a long time, he was rethinking his decision to leave. But he feared that had more to do with Trice than it did with the medical practice or Luce.

Still, he had made his plans, and he wouldn't let a woman he had just met derail them. Dr. Johannsson's death had done that once. Drake had no intention of letting that happen again.

"Will you tell me what it was like growing up here? Do you have brothers and sisters?" Trice watched him with expectation.

"I do. My sister lives in Reykjavík, and I have a brother who lives across the island in a small village. My parents moved a couple of years ago when my father was transferred to Reykjavík. That's when Luce became my responsibility. We've always been close. I do hate the idea of leaving her."

"It's nice to know you have a family. Everyone should have someone." She couldn't keep the sadness out of her voice.

Drake looked at her with sympathy. "You have no sense of what that is like, do you?"

"No, not really. Friendships and working relationships but no true connection."

"As much as I might complain, I'm glad to have my family, here. So many of us from Iceland are connected." He was quiet for a moment. "You know, it just occurs to me there is someone I've heard of living up here that you might like to interview for your research project. Let me make a few contacts, and we can possibly visit her before we leave." His gaze met hers. "If you'd like to? It looks as if we're going to be stuck here for the night. Maybe this evening, we could go do an interview."

"That would be wonderful." She sat straighter. The blanket slipped.

Drake took the chance to enjoy the view. He couldn't help but be disappointed when she adjusted it and curtained his show. The eagerness in Trice's eyes made his heart expand with pleasure. He had put that look on her face. "Let me make some calls, and I'll let you know if we can make the trip. I will also see if one of the women on the rescue squad has any spare pants. I have a shirt you can wear, but the pants, I'm afraid, will swallow you whole. You hang out here, and I'll be back with clothes and information." He grabbed his coat and started for the door.

Trice still sat on the sofa warming herself when

Drake reentered with the damp wind and rain behind him. He quickly closed the door. "I wish I could say the weather is better, but it doesn't feel like it. We are a go, and I had good luck with clothes." He held up a bag.

"Thanks for thinking of everything."

"Before you dress, we need to get some cream on your back. I saw you wince a moment ago."

She looked at him. "Are you sure I can't handle it on my own?"

"Please just let me see to it." Drake went to his pack and removed a small jar. He sat beside her. "Let the blanket down." He tugged the material out of the way. This time he did take a moment to admire her lovely back. The urge to kiss the ridge of her shoulder almost overcame him. He closed his eyes, refocused his thoughts. This wasn't the time or the place.

"Hey, what's taking so long?"

"Just opening the jar." He lifted the cream with his index finger and slowly ran it over her spine. Trice's muscles rippled. Her skin was like touching velvet, warm, plush and elegant.

"That feels good." Trice's voice held a deep, sexy timbre that didn't encourage his control.

This was a worse idea than he had feared it might be. He took another moment to gather himself. He would and could get through this.

"All done." With a sigh, he covered her back with the blanket. He quickly stood, moving away.

"Go get dressed. We must leave soon to be there on time."

That was all it took to get Trice moving. "Give me five minutes."

She returned wearing a T-shirt with his shirt buttoned over it and tied at her waist. The jeans he had borrowed from the female EMT were snug and hugged Trice's curves in a provocative way.

Drake swallowed hard. He could do this. Luce was right. Trice deserved better than being pursued by someone who had no intention of being around next week. Based on what she'd said, she had experienced more than her fair share of that in life already.

"Let me get my boots on and I'll be ready to go," she said.

"By the way, I was very impressed with your professionalism and your abilities today. Not everyone would've done what you did."

"Sometimes we have to do what scares us because it has to be done."

"Like flying?" He grinned.

"Yeah. And other things."

Was she trying to make a point? "You understand that better than most."

"I guess I do."

"That doesn't make you any less amazing." He stepped toward the door.

"Thank you. Enough about that. Who is this

person we are going to see?" She followed him out, grabbing her coat on the way.

"An elder woman. She knows Luce. I visited her when I was a child. She is related to almost everyone around here. She might give you some names of people who have had HEP. Her seal of approval will take you a long way in gaining information."

"She does sound like an excellent person to get to know." Trice pulled on her coat.

He shrugged into his jacket. "Hallveig said she'd be glad to see us in about an hour. I made arrangements for us to borrow one of the rescue trucks."

"You think of everything, don't you?"

"Not everything, but I try to be thorough." That was one of the skills he had been told made him a good surgeon.

"That's what makes you such a good doctor." Trice had recognized it, and she hadn't even seen him with a scalpel.

"Thank you. You are starting to embarrass me. We've had an emotional day, so I guess we're going to brag to each other for the rest of it."

Trice laughed as she ran for the truck. She called over the hood as she climbed in, grinning, "If we don't, who's going to?"

He like the sound of her laugh. It made him want to join her in the humor. "On that note, let's get going. We have a drive ahead of us."

"Is it a long way?"

He settled behind the steering wheel. "Not so much distance. More like windy, steep roads. It just takes time to maneuver."

Half an hour later, Drake drove around another switchback. "I have only been this way once, and it was a long time ago."

"I am not complaining. I'm just glad for this opportunity. Is there anything I should know about Hallveig?"

"She's not exactly the spiritual leader of the area, but she's right up there. She's around ninety years old but doesn't know for sure how old she is. She knows most people around here, and she keeps the old Icelandic ways that have been handed down."

Another half an hour later with it still raining and the wind whipping around them, Drake pulled onto a narrow path and parked on the side of the road. "We have to walk from here."

"How did you even know where to pull over?" She looked around with eyes wide and mouth open.

He enjoyed looking at Trice when she had that bright-eyed, anything-is-possible look on her face. It made him want to see things the same way. "I got very specific instructions. Large tree with rocks in the curve."

"Interesting road signs." Trice climbed out of the truck and closed the door.

He met her at the front of the truck. "They aren't that unusual around here."

"Those I'll have to get used to. So, Hallveig lives all the way out here by herself."

"She does, which makes her that much more interesting. Despite where she lives, she knows everything going on for miles." He caught her elbow when she slipped.

"She must be fascinating."

They made their way down a single-file path with only a few trees.

"Why aren't there more trees?" Trice asked.

"Because they were all cut down and used for building houses and keeping warm through the years of settlement. Now we have a program to plant trees. It's working, but it's a slow process. It will take time to correct what we did in the past. Now we're looking for other ways to have what we need without cutting down trees."

"That makes sense."

They navigated the narrow path between two large boulders. A small house came into view. One that was little more than a shack. No light shone from within.

"I thought you said she is expecting us." She looked at him with a wrinkled brow of concern.

"She is." Drake stood before the door, giving it a light knock. He didn't want to disappoint Trice. The idea of being her hero appealed.

Time passed to the point he feared either Hallveig wasn't home or something was wrong. As he had made the decision to enter to check on her, the door was opened. A twisted, stoop-shouldered woman he hardly recognized stood there.

"I was expecting you." She didn't wait for them to respond. Instead, she turned and started back into the dim room.

The house held only a few pieces of furniture. Just the necessities. The glow from the fire gave off light along with one oil lamp sitting in the middle of a table in the center of the room. The bed was located on one side of the house and the kitchen on the other.

"Close the door and sit." The command came as little more than a growl.

"I'm Dr. Drake Stevansson. Years ago I came to see you with my grandmother, Luce."

"I remember you." She studied Trice as if she were something interesting under a microscope. "And you are?"

Trice stepped forward. "I'm Dr. Beatrice Shell."

"The new doctor."

Trice held eye contact. "Yes."

"Sit." Hallveig waved a gnarled hand up and down. She sat in a well-worn chair near the fire.

"Thank you for seeing us," Trice said. She pulled a wooden chair from the table, faced the woman and lowered herself into it.

Drake chose to stand on the other side of the fireplace from Hallveig.

Trice didn't appear taken aback by the woman's abrupt manner. "The reason I am here is that I am doing a medical study on people carrying the HEP gene. Are you familiar with the genetic disorder?"

Hallveig nodded.

"I understand you know everything that happens around here and everyone." Trice watched Hallveig intently.

She nodded but offered no encouragement to talk.

Trice moved to the edge of her seat. "Do you know anyone who has HEP or has been diagnosed with it?"

The question hung in the air for a minute. "I had it as a child. I recovered with a few scars. My brother had many."

"May I ask you some more questions and draw a small amount of blood?" Trice pulled a notebook out of the pocket of her coat.

Apparently, she had taken a few minutes while he was gone earlier to prepare for the meeting. Trice continued to impress him.

"Questions, yes. Blood, I'm not sure." Hallveig leaned back in her chair and picked up her knitting.

Trice leaned forward, looking earnest. "I could make it just a finger stick, if you would allow?"

Hallveig took so long to nod, Drake worried she might not.

"I would also like to talk to members of your family if I may. I would ask them the same questions I am going to ask you." Trice almost vibrated with her excitement.

Hallveig looked at Drake.

He nodded. "You can trust her, Hallveig."

The woman nodded too. "I heard what she did at the falls."

Drake smiled. How it had reached the old woman all the way up here so fast, he might never understand. "Yes, she was impressive."

Hallveig's attention returned to Trice. "I will agree. But I must ask my family if they agree."

"Will you tell them to contact me at the clinic?"

"I will."

Over the next few minutes, Drake stood quietly by while Trice conducted her interview. Once again, he was impressed by her consideration and scholarly manner. More than that, she was patient and kind with the older woman. Where had Trice been all his life?

"That's it for the questions," Trice announced. "Thank you so much, Hallveig. I only need one more thing. Just a little bit of blood." She pulled a blood sample kit out of her pocket.

Drake grinned. Trice used that pocket like a magician used a hat to do a trick. What else did she have in there?

"Hallveig, may I see your finger?"

The older woman offered her hand.

"There will be a little prick and squeeze." Trice suctioned the drop of blood into a small plastic tube and closed the top. It went into the pocket. She then carefully placed a Band-Aid over the spot. "That's it."

With the efficiency he had come to expect from Trice, she finished with Hallveig. "Thank you so much for doing this."

The woman nodded.

Now it was his turn. "Hallveig, when was the last time you had a checkup?"

"I don't know." She continued with her knitting.

"That long. Would you mind if I had a look at you since I am here?"

"I don't need one." The woman's hands didn't slow down. She wasn't going to agree without some coaxing.

"Would you please do it for me? It won't take but a minute. It will not hurt at all. I'll just have a quick listen to you."

She considered him long and hard, then nodded.

Drake smiled. He looked at Trice. "May I borrow your stethoscope?"

She reached in her pocket, found the instrument and handed it to him.

Minutes later he pronounced, "Hallveig, you are in remarkable health. May we all be doing as well as you."

Hallveig gave him a toothless grin. "I knew as much."

Drake returned her smile, then winked at Trice before handing back her stethoscope. "I bet you did. We must go now."

Trice stood.

"Dr. Stevansson leaves soon," Hallveig stated more than questioned.

"I do." Drake placed his hand on the woman's shoulder briefly. He was no longer saying that with the confidence he once had.

"Hallveig, do you ever come to Seydisfjordur?" Trice asked quietly.

"Once a year. It is a long way for me."

"I understand. I hope you come while I am still there. It would be lovely to see you again. You will talk to your family?"

"I will." Hallveig narrowed her eyes as she looked at Trice once more. "You have the Viking ancestry."

Trice smiled. "I do. Somewhere. Sometime."

"Come closer," Hallveig demanded. The woman took her chin, gripped it, then moved it back and forth. "You are a Bjonsson."

"What?"

Drake said, "That's a last name. We put *daughter* or *son* on the end of the father's name. The Bjonssons are well known in this area. There's even one in Seydisfjordur."

"I am a Bjonsson." The pleasure in Trice's

voice said it all. Her world had been made complete. In an odd way, he wished he had been the one to put that pleased look on her face.

"Are you sure?" Trice asked with tears forming in her eyes.

The woman nodded.

"I would never doubt Hallveig," Drake assured Trice with a squeeze on her shoulder.

Hallveig looked perplexed. "She did not know?"

He smiled at the old woman. "No, she did not know. You have made her very happy."

Trice gave the fragile woman a gentle hug. "Thank you."

Hallveig put her hands on Trice's shoulders and looked into her face. "You are good. We will be glad you are one of us."

Drake let Trice exit before him. "Thank you, Hallveig."

"Young man." She stopped him.

Fear washed through him at her tone.

"You do not know your heart or your place. You think on that before you make a mistake."

# CHAPTER SIX

TRICE STOOD IN dumbfounded silence outside Hallveig's house. She couldn't believe it. She was a Bjonsson. She had family. No matter how distant. Roots. A history.

Hallveig pronounced it with such confidence. Could it be true?

Drake stood close beside her. "Are you okay?"

She looked into his concerned eyes and gave him a huge smile. "I'm better than okay." She wrapped her arms around his neck. "I have family. Real, breathing family."

His hands came to her waist. "Yes, you do."

"I'm so excited. I can't believe it." She hugged him tighter, then pulled away.

"Isn't that part of why you wanted to come to Iceland, to find family?"

She liked being held by Drake. In fact, she wanted him to hold her more. "It is, but I never really thought I would find anyone that might belong to me."

He chuckled. "We better get out of this weather

and back to the truck or you may be too sick to find them."

"Never." She started down the path. "This has been the best day. Do you know the Bjonsson who lives in Seydisfjordur?"

"I have met him." His tone was flat and dry.

She stopped walking and studied Drake. "That didn't sound very encouraging."

Drake twisted his mouth. "He isn't the most approachable person."

All the air went out of her lungs. "Oh. You don't think he will speak to me?"

"I'm just afraid you might not get a very warm welcome." Drake took her elbow and directed her on down the path.

"I'll take my chances." She would get the man to at least see her. Make him understand how important to her it was to meet him.

They reached the truck. Trice climbed in, shivering.

Drake slid behind the steering wheel, then turned a knob. "It'll be warm in here in a few minutes."

Trice huddled close to the warm air coming out of the vent. "By the by, I'm sorry I didn't even think about giving Hallveig a checkup. All I was concerned about was what I wanted."

"That's what we went for. I just thought since we were there, she needed to be seen. We've had more than a big day. Let's go back to the cabin and get some rest. We'll leave at daylight if the weather will let us. I'll see about us visiting old man Bjonsson when we get home."

That's what he thought of Seydisfjordur. As home. Soon he would have a new home. A new life. A new career. He would prove to himself and anyone else watching that was where he belonged. He would keep his promise to himself and his grandfather to help people. But wasn't he helping people here? Hallveig's words came to mind. *You do not know your heart or your place.*

Trice rubbed her hands together. "You know you don't have to take what little time you have left in town seeing about me. Give me some directions and I will go see him."

Drake looked at her. "I like spending time with you."

"OK, thank you."

"After we get back and see things settled around the clinic, we'll drive up the valley to visit him. I just don't want you to get your hopes up. He's not what you would call a family man. In fact, he has run all of them off that I know of."

"Oh, then he may not welcome me." The idea made her sad.

He glanced at her, then returned his attention to the road.

Less than an hour later and not soon enough for her aching back, Drake pulled into the road by the cabin. "I sure would like to know how our two patients are doing."

"So would I. Would you like to go to the restaurant for dinner and see what we can find out?"

"That sounds good."

Drake drove along a road she didn't recognize, then parked in front of a long building. "Since there's only light rain, we'll leave the truck here and take the path back to the cabin."

"If anybody's learned their lesson about the importance of staying on a path, that's me." She climbed out of the truck, taking a moment to stretch her back.

"I can't say it enough. You did impressive work this morning. Far above what you were expected to do." He held the door for her to enter the building.

"I think it was more about me being scared than anything." She stepped by him to stop in what was obviously the lobby of the resort.

"Many people don't do things because they're scared." A low fire burned in a rock fireplace. He started down a hall.

She joined him. "Are you scared of something?"

"Yeah. I'm afraid of never having the chance to do what I love."

Trice regarded him. "Surgery?"

"Yeah. I am so close to finishing my training."

He stopped at the door of a room filled with tables and chairs.

"Why did you go into medicine?"

"Because my grandfather died when there wasn't someone close who could perform surgery. He was too sick to fly, and the road would have taken too long. I watched him suffer. I made up my mind then that I'd become a surgeon so others wouldn't have to watch their loved ones die."

A woman came to show them to a table.

"But if you leave, won't the people around here be in the same situation?" She weaved between tables of people to their spot.

When they had settled in their chairs, Drake leaned over the table toward her. "Leave it to you to ask the difficult questions. No, because I have no place to do surgery, no theater. The clinic would need to be enlarged. There's no money for that."

"I can understand that, but I can also understand the significance of what you do here."

Drake had obviously made up his mind about leaving. It wasn't her place to try to change it. Even if she could. He deserved his chance at his dream just as she was getting hers. Yet it still made her sad to think of him leaving. She would miss him. Too much.

The woman taking their order brought her attention back to the here and now. Their discussion went to subjects more general over dinner. They strolled back to the cabin.

Trice pulled her coat off and hung it up before turning her back to the smoldering fire. "I'm glad our patients are doing so well."

"I am as well. I just wish you hadn't gotten hurt in the process."

She twisted her back. It had eased since they got out of the truck. "It's not that bad, but I know I'll be sleeping on my stomach."

Drake made a noise that sounded like a groan.

She considered him, eyes narrowed. "Are you okay?"

"Yeah. Fine." He didn't look at her. "I should put some more cream on your back. Otherwise, you'll have a difficult time sleeping the night through. I'll build the fire while you get ready for me to do that."

"Are you planning to stay here tonight?"

"I was. Unless you have a problem with it. We are lucky to get this cabin. All of them are taken with the rescue crew and tourists. I can see if I can bunk with someone else if you aren't comfortable with me being here. I promise to be a perfect gentleman."

"What if I don't want you to be a gentleman?" That popped out. Was her subconscious speaking for her now? What would be wrong with them enjoying each other while they could? Would that be so awful? He would be gone soon. She gave him a sideways look to see what his reaction was to that. Had she shocked him?

Drake stopped midmovement to look at her. "Trice, you need to think carefully about what you are saying."

She faced him. "I know what I'm saying. I'm attracted to you. I thought maybe you were to me too."

He looked at her for a moment. Saying nothing.

That was a gamble that didn't pay off. She started toward the bedroom. "I'm sorry. Am I being too blunt? Just forget I said anything."

"Trice."

"Yes." She glanced back.

His voice dropped low. "You didn't misread anything."

She continued into the bedroom with a smile on her lips. A few minutes later she called, "Ready." Trice had slid under the covers to her waist, her back bare. She hurt and looked forward to having Drake's fingers moving across her in a gentle glide. A creak in the floor told her Drake had entered.

"Scoot to the middle some."

She did as he requested, being careful not to show more of herself than necessary.

The bed dipped. Drake sat on the edge of the mattress. "This still looks painful."

"Yes, Mother Hen," she grumbled.

"There's nothing wrong with being careful." He smoothed cream over her skin.

She shivered from the coolness of the cream, or Drake's touch, she wasn't sure which. "Never said there was."

"Yet you're making fun of me."

She considered him over her shoulder. "I do appreciate your concern."

His gaze met hers. It was soft, caressing and enquiring. His fingers journeyed down her back. She quaked. He blinked, and the look disappeared. He quickly stood. "You need to get some good rest. I'll see you in the morning."

She held the blanket to her as she rolled so she could see him. "Where are you planning to sleep?"

"I'll take the sofa. You are in pain."

"But there's plenty of room in this bed."

"You do know what will happen if I do that, and you are in no shape for that amount of activity."

She couldn't let him sleep on an uncomfortable sofa. "Don't make me feel guilty about sleeping in this comfortable bed. You've had a hard day, and you need your rest too." Why was she pushing this? "Look, there's plenty of room for both of us. We're adults. I believe we can control our actions." She hoped she spoke for them both, especially herself. "Don't we have to be up early?"

Drake looked at her long enough that she had

become convinced he wasn't going to take her up on the invitation.

"All right. I will, but if I disrupt your sleep or hurt your back for some reason, then I'm off to the sofa."

He headed for the bathroom.

By the time Drake returned, she'd pulled on a T-shirt and settled on her stomach. She was aware of the dip in the mattress as he climbed in beside her.

Drake faced away from Trice, trying not to move until his muscles had locked into place. He would be sore in the morning from trying not to touch her. Sleeping on the floor might have been more comfortable than having a warm woman next to him and being unable to touch her. His life kept taking turns he hadn't expected. And currently didn't enjoy.

*You do not know your heart or your place.* Those words echoed again. "Trice, about what we were talking about earlier."

"Mmm."

"What do you think we should do about it?" He sure knew what he wanted to do. But he wanted to hear her say it.

"I thought a hot no-strings fling as long as you are here would be superb."

Drake's stomach muscles tightened at the idea. His manhood twitched in anticipation.

"We aren't going the same direction in life," she said. "I don't see either one of us settling down anytime soon. We have plans we want to accomplish. Let's make it clean and simple so that when you leave, we part as friends."

He winced. Had she been so hurt in the past that she didn't want any strings? Her background had made her that way. She had no ties to anything, and his entire life was filled with strings. He had to give her credit. Her fortitude impressed him.

If she could put what she wanted ahead of everything, then he could too. "I like that plan. But not tonight. I want you feeling better and in no pain."

She rolled, and her fingertips brushed along his bicep.

His hand stopped hers. "You rest, and we will talk about it more tomorrow."

"Promise?"

"You can count on it."

Minutes later, he heard her even breathing. She was asleep.

A groan awakened him. There was movement from Trice's side of the bed. She rolled to her back, yelped, then returned to where she had been, releasing another groan.

His hand hadn't touched her skin before he felt

the heat. Trice had a fever. He rested the back of his hand on her forehead. It was a high one.

She relaxed for a moment.

Drake turned on the bedside lamp, then went to the main room and retrieved his medical backpack. After finding his thermometer, he ran it over her head from ear to ear. The reading flashing in the tiny screen was one hundred two degrees. He searched for the fever-reducing medicine and shook out a couple of tablets before he filled a glass with water.

Placing the glass on the table beside the bed, he took a seat beside Trice. "Trice, you have a fever. Can you sit up and take some medicine?"

She rolled her head back and forth.

He slipped an arm under her shoulders, being careful not to touch her injury, and lifted her forward.

She moaned and opened her red, glassy eyes. "I was having a wonderful dream. You were kissing me."

He wished he had been. Trying to ignore her statement and his urge to do just that, he said, "You need to sit up and take these. Open your mouth."

She did.

He quickly brought the water to her lips. She eagerly drank. Some of it dribbled down her chin and dropped on her chest. "Finish the water, sweetheart."

Trice did as he instructed.

He dabbed the stray water from her chin with the sheet. "Now, lie back. I'm going to get a cool compress for your head. You'll be fine in the morning."

"Don't go." Her eyelids slowly closed.

"I'll be right back." He hurried to the bathroom, found a washcloth, wet it and returned to Trice.

She lay back on the pillow, her eyes still closed. Drake placed the cloth across her forehead.

Trice sighed. "Feels good. Back hurts."

"I know, sweetheart. I know. I need to have a look at it. Can you roll over?"

"I don't want to." Her eyes fluttered open.

"Your back won't hurt as bad if you get off it." She muttered something he couldn't understand. "I'll help you." He pulled at the blankets. All she wore was the T-shirt and light pink panties, but he wouldn't allow himself to dwell on that fact. He raised one shoulder and pushed her hip, encouraging her to shift. She moved to her stomach without a noise.

Drake lifted her shirt and winced. The bruises had turned darker. Trice said nothing and didn't move.

"I'll need to check things in the morning. Try to get some sleep." He carefully lowered her shirt. Taking the rag to the bath once more, he ran it under cool water and placed it on her forehead.

Trice felt cooler now. Turning off the bedside lamp, he lay down.

Trice took his hand. Her hot breath flowed over his arm. "You're a nice man."

Drake couldn't see her clearly in the dim light. He smiled. Had there been no one who took care of her when she was sick?

"Sorry I woke you." She wiggled next to him.

"Not a problem. Hush now. You need to sleep."

She pushed into his side. "You do too. I'm cold."

Her fever was breaking. He put his arm beneath her neck. She rested her head on his chest. He was careful not to touch her back.

Her lips touched his chest. "Thank you for taking care of me. I wish I felt better."

He groaned. "Trice, don't do that. You are not up to it, and I can't resist you if you don't help me."

She wiggled against his side again and sighed.

Trice had fallen asleep, but that wouldn't be happening for him for a long time to come. He had been trying to keep some space between them, but that wasn't working. Trice had a way of pulling him closer. His fingertips brushed the top of the curve of her hip. He hadn't anticipated being shaken by the instantaneous combustion between them in such a short period of time.

He wanted her. It was time for him to accept that, but he didn't have any business letting himself fall for her. Her back hurt, and he planned to leave in five days. His thoughts had gone crazy since Trice had arrived. No matter what he did, they circled around to her.

That would end when he left. His emotions would settle down again. He'd get involved in his work and adjust to life in London. Would she even want him to stay? If she did, would he be just another person on the long list of people who had let her down?

Drake reminded himself of that idea throughout the night while he held Trice. Somehow, he didn't think it would be that easy anymore. He didn't want to leave Trice alone. And oddly, leaving Seydisfjordur didn't have the same appeal. Luce was right. It didn't seem fair to Trice. Yet he had to. There were commitments to honor. His dream to pursue. Returning to Seydisfjordur had only been a detour.

Trice woke to the warm reality of a hard body next to hers. She lay on her side, and a heavy arm rested across her waist.

A soft snore came from above her head.

She opened her eyelids just enough to look over the plane of Drake's chest covered by material.

Another snore made her grin. She looked up, seeing the dark shadow along his jaw. She really liked his jaw. Her fingers twitched to trace that dark line, but she stopped them. She shouldn't start anything that she wasn't physically capable of carrying through with.

She needed her life to move forward. There was a chance she might find a family member, a distant one, but family none the less. She couldn't become wrapped up in a man who would leave and never look back. That wasn't the type of relationship she wanted or needed. She wanted a sturdy and healthy one. There had been enough partial relationships in her life already. But to spend a few lovely hours in his arms with no strings attached would make for nice memories. "Drake."

His eyelids fluttered. His fingertips brushed the curve of her breast as he removed his arm. Looking at her, he said, "Hey."

The temptation to kiss him right then grabbed her when his sexy morning voice flowed over her.

"Did you sleep any last night?" He studied her.

She yawned. "Best ever. How about you?"

Drake's warm, caressing look found and held hers. "Best ever. How's the back?"

"Hurts."

"Roll and let me have a look." He shifted, making the mattress dip.

"I don't think this—"

"Trice, let me see."

She did as he said. Satisfaction went through her when she heard the tight intake of his breath.

She hadn't bothered to pull the covers up. Her bikini underwear was clearly in view.

Drake pushed her T-shirt up her back in a slow, revealing way. The sizzle in the air made her breath catch. She remained still.

"Trice." His voice sounded hoarse.

She said softly, "Yes?"

"You may want to breathe. I don't want you to pass out." A teasing note surrounded the words.

She rolled enough that she could see his face. "I'm breathing." She took a deep breath, letting it out slowly. Drake's eyes widened and focused on her breasts.

"Trice." His tone matched a father disciplining a child. "I'm trying very hard to remain a doctor here. You are not making it easy. Now stop playing and let me see your back."

She settled on her stomach again, pleasure filling her. Drake struggled with their attraction as much as she did.

"This looks better than it did last night." The tip of a finger ran down the length of her back to the dip of her waist. Cool, dry lips rested a second on the back of her shoulder. In a low voice Drake said, "Two can play the same game."

She rolled to her side. Her gaze locked with his. "Do you really want to play?"

Drake climbed out of bed and regarded her. "I'm leaving. You're staying."

"You didn't answer my question."

"Which one? Do I want you? Yes. You are the sexiest woman I've ever seen. The most amazing one. The bravest. The most beautiful. Hell yeah, I want you."

"You mean that?" Did he really feel that way?

He looked into her eyes. "Every word of it."

Trice slipped from the bed, not caring about the skimpy clothing she wore. Walking to Drake, she put her arms around his neck and kissed him. "Thank you for that. No one has ever said anything like that to me."

Drake gently placed his hands on her waist, but the tension in his body said he held himself under control. His mouth found hers. He pulled her secure against him. His manhood stood strong and thick between them. His tongue ran along the seam of her lips. That was all the encouragement she needed to open for him. Drake invaded with the eagerness of a person thirsty for water. Their tongues tangled. She gripped his shoulders. His hands remained on her waist, but his fingers tightened. How like him to always be mindful of her injury.

She'd been kissed before, but none had been like this one. This went to her soul, captured her.

Drake cupped her butt and lifted. She wrapped her legs around his waist. Her center rested against the stiffness of him, making her tingle with desire. She whimpered. His thumbs slid beneath the elastic of her panties.

A knock on the door stopped any further exploration. Drake's mouth left hers. His heated eyes held want, disappointment and something she couldn't define. He let her deliberately slide down his body.

"I should get that." He stepped away, jerked on his jeans, and headed for the door.

She heard Drake talking to another man but couldn't make out the words. Quickly she pulled on her clothes, taking special care with her shirt, not applying too much pressure to her back.

Drake returned. "We need to get moving. That was one of the rescue squad. They are leaving and wanted to know if we needed a ride to the plane. I told them we would appreciate one. We shouldn't make them wait."

"I'll be ready in ten minutes. Will that do?"

He didn't look at her as he spoke. "That will do. The sky looks nice and clear. The flight home should be smooth."

She shuddered.

Drake narrowed his eyes. "What was that for?"

"The thought of going up in an airplane again." She pulled on her pants.

He pulled on his shirt. "You know, you could hurt my feelings."

She wasn't clear if he was teasing or not. "I don't mean to. It's just that I'm not a big fan of flying in general."

"Or my plane in particular. Yet you jumped

at the chance to hang ten meters above roaring water and rocks."

"I didn't jump at the idea. I did what had to be done." Why did she feel the need to defend herself? He'd been there. Knew the situation.

He stepped to her, his eyes predatory.

Would he kiss her again? She would like it if he did.

"And you were magnificent. I was proud of you." He placed his hands on her shoulders and gave her a kiss on the forehead. "Now to see if you do as well getting home."

She sagged with disappointment when he moved away.

"Do you have everything?" He looked around the room.

"Yep. I didn't come with much."

"You will need your jacket." He pulled it off the back of a chair and handed it to her. "It's time to go home."

She hadn't thought about it, but she was going home. Seydisfjordur was as much her home in a little over a week as any other place she had ever been. "Yes, let's go home."

An hour later, Drake had the engine warmed up and prepared for takeoff. He pushed the throttle forward, and the plane ran down the runway.

As he made movements with his hands and feet that were now second nature to him, he was aware of Trice trying to cover her anxiety. It wasn't working. She held her breath, and her fingers bit into the seat cushion.

"I wish you'd settle back over there. It's a beautiful day for flying." He turned the plane toward the east.

"So you say," she grumbled.

"Look out at how beautiful it is." For some reason he wanted her to enjoy flying.

"I can't yet."

"For a woman who hung over the side of a cliff for hours yesterday, I can't understand why you're so scared being in an airplane with me."

"It's not your flying."

"Thank goodness. Would you like to fly over the waterfall where we were yesterday?"

It took her a moment, but she said, "Yes. I would like to see it."

He made a turn.

"Wow, I didn't mean for you to do that." Her hand gripped his arm.

His look met hers. "I'll take care of you. Now, be looking down, because here it comes."

"Oh, wow."

She let go of him. He missed her touch immediately. "This is one of the most beautiful waterfalls in Iceland."

"Look at those boulders below. I'm glad I didn't know of their size yesterday. You might have had to push me over the side."

He had known. That had been one of the reasons he'd not wanted her to go. "It is deep. This is a wonderful tourist spot, but it has to be respected. It's also dangerous."

"I'm going to read up on it when we get home."

At least she no longer looked terrified and was speaking to him normally. "You might enjoy a book I have about Iceland's history and special sights. You need to visit some of these places if and when you have a chance."

Her face turned eager, eyes bright. "I'd love to read the book. I promise to leave it with Luce to return to you, or I could even mail it."

"You don't have to do either of those. I would like to give it to you." He made a banking turn to the left, leaving the falls behind them. He loved seeing her enthusiasm about what he considered commonplace. It made him see the sights in a different light. With wonder and anticipation. Being with Trice had him experiencing what he'd always known but with renewed pleasure.

"Thank you. That's nice of you. I will cherish it."

He like the idea of her having something that had been his.

They continued toward Seydisfjordur. Drake did a few subtle dips and turns so Trice could see the mountains.

"I love the snow-tipped mountains," she said as much to herself as him.

Drake chuckled. "After six months or more, you may not see them the same way. You'll be looking for spring like everyone else around here."

"But not you. You will be in England with rain."

They had reached the fjord. He flew over the water. Trice's fingers turned white as she held the door handle. The tires touched the runway with a screech, and they rolled toward the building.

Trice released her grip and breathed a sigh of relief. "Were you trying to impress me just now with those maneuvers?"

"What if I was?" He pulled the plane to a stop.

"Why would you?"

He looked at her. "Isn't that what a guy does when he likes a girl?"

Pink spotted her cheeks. "Drake, are you flirting with me?"

He grinned. "About ninety percent of the time."

# CHAPTER SEVEN

TRICE CLIMBED FROM the plane as Drake exited the other side. Relieved to have her feet back on the ground, she had still enjoyed being with Drake. She especially enjoyed him flirting with her. And most of all his kiss.

"I know you must be tired. I'll drop you by Luce's and head over to the clinic to see if there's anything I need to do."

"I work there. I should be there as well." She pulled her bag out of the storage compartment.

He grabbed his too and closed the door. "You are a tough person to be nice to. I might have made a few more dips and turns if I had known you could be so contrary."

"You would have done that?" She looked at him with a mock shocked face that included an open mouth.

He shrugged. "Sure. I have already admitted I was showing off some."

She glared at him. "If you were trying to impress me, that wasn't the way."

He stepped closer, watching her. "If I wanted to impress you, how would I go about doing that?"

"I don't know. Maybe by taking me out for a nighttime picnic to watch the stars. Something that was less likely to make my stomach roll."

"Then how about joining me tonight? I know just the place. And just the sky to find them in. Wear warm clothes and the socks I loaned you."

"Okay. I'll take that dare, or date, whichever you're making it." They started toward his truck.

"I like the idea of a date." A look of satisfaction came across his face.

They climbed into his truck.

She smiled. "I like the idea of a date as well."

Excitement he'd not experienced in a long time ran through him. Just the idea of spending time with Trice had a way of doing that. He made the short drive to the clinic.

They were only there five minutes before they had three patients. They were simple matters of a child with an upset stomach, an older woman complaining of a bad cold, and a man who had a bunion that needed attention. They divided the cases between the two of them and soon finished.

After yesterday's adventure, every problem seemed easier.

Trice hadn't complained of her back hurting despite her discomfort in the plane. When she returned home, she would give it some attention.

She had almost finished cleaning the exam room when Drake came to the door.

"Your turn."

"What?" She faced him.

"It's time for me to give your back a look. I saw the way you shifted in the plane seat. You were in pain." He entered the room.

"Not pain. Uncomfortable. I'll look at it when I get home."

"You know you can't reach it if you need to care for it. Now stop arguing and let me see." He stood beside the gurney.

She huffed. "I think you're enjoying this."

He grinned. "I think you might be right. I do like looking at your lovely back, but right now I'll focus on giving a medical evaluation."

She turned her back to him and lifted her shirt.

"You will be glad to know it's much improved. You have a rainbow of colors. You can pull your shirt down now." He stepped away from her.

She did and turned to face him. "Satisfied?"

"With your recovery, yes." He walked toward the door. "I think we have everything settled here if you want to go home. I'll be leaving in a half an hour as soon as I put in the reports."

"I can do those and close up." She didn't want him to see her as a slacker.

"Trice, wouldn't you like to get out of those clothes?"

She looked down at what she'd been wearing

for the better part of two days. "Are you saying you would like me to freshen up before you see me again tonight?"

His look remained on her. "I don't think it would hurt either one of us to clean up."

"Okay. I'll go. What time should I expect you?"

He stopped on the way to the office. "Eleven o'clock too early?"

"Wow, that late?"

"It takes a long time to get dark here this time of year."

"I will be ready." The idea of seeing him again made her giddy.

"You sure you're up to it tonight? It can wait until tomorrow."

She was eager to spend as much time with him as she could. "If you're up to it, I'm up to it. I might have another social engagement if we wait."

They both laughed.

"This isn't a place where there's a nightclub on every corner or even a movie theater."

Like he would have in London. "I'd rather look at the stars anyway."

"Then I'll see you in a few hours. Don't forget to wear warm clothes."

She was curious now. "Where're we going?"

"That's my surprise."

Drake was astonished he hadn't seen Lucc. He expected her there with her disapproving look.

A tinge of guilt filled him. But he was an adult and so was Trice. They didn't need Luce to make their decisions for them.

Still, he suspected she was right. This probably wouldn't end well for one or both of them. He held his head high and walked to Trice's door. Knocking, he waited until she opened it.

"You still feel up to an evening out?"

"You bet. Let me get my coat." She went back into the house and returned with the coat in hand.

He led her to the truck and helped her in. Five minutes later, they were on the road leading into the valley.

"Shouldn't we be going up the mountain?" Trice looked ahead of them.

"You just sit back. I'll do the driving. We're higher than you think."

After another two miles, he turned off the paved road and drove along a gravel one. A few minutes later, she realized how high they had gone, causing her to hold on to the door handle.

Drake glanced at her. "High enough for you?"

She continued to focus on the outside view. "I'd have to say yes."

Drake chuckled, pulling to the side of the road and parking the truck.

"We're stopping here?" She looked around them as if expecting more.

He opened the door and hopped out. "This is where we're going."

"Oh."

He wanted to show her the best of Iceland. She said she loved the stars, and there was no better place to see them than here. The sky would be a regular festival of lights tonight. This was the perfect place to see the show. Once again, he had to remind himself this wasn't some relationship where he had to impress the girl. Yet he wanted Trice to remember him well. Why was it so important that she did?

She climbed down from the truck to meet him. "This view is amazing without stars."

"I think so." He reached in the back for the picnic basket, blanket and plastic ground cover. Closing the door, he said, "This way."

"Can I help you carry something?"

He handed her the blanket. "Up for a little stroll?"

"Sure."

He led the way up a path. They walked for ten minutes until they came to an open field. By this time, it was dusk. They were surrounded by nothing but sky.

"I didn't think it could get any better, but it has."

Drake knew from the sound of Trice's voice he'd impressed her. He liked that idea. What would her reaction be in a little while? It was fun showing his homeland to someone who appreciated it.

"How did you find this place?" she asked.

"It wasn't too hard. My house is just right over there." He pointed behind him toward a rise.

She gave him a suspicious look. "So what was all the driving and walking about, then, if your house is right over there?"

Drake shrugged. "Because it was the easiest way to get to this spot." He kicked a couple of rocks out of the way, then flipped the plastic sheet out, laying it on the ground. Taking the blanket from her, he positioned it over the plastic. In the middle, he placed the picnic basket. From the basket he pulled a candle in a glass. He lit it and set it to the side.

"Join me? The light show will start in a few minutes." He sat with his legs crossed.

Trice joined him on the blanket, a grin on her face. "Why, Doctor, this is impressive."

"I'm glad you like it." He opened the basket and removed food containers, placing them within reach. Last he took out plates, utensils, wine and glasses.

"You thought of everything."

"I tried." He served their plates, handing her one.

She tasted each item. "This is wonderful."

"Thank you." He bowed his head.

She took another bite. "Did you make it?"

"No, I asked Marta at the café to put something together, so I can't take credit for it." He opened a container.

"It's a relief to know you aren't perfect at everything." She ate a spoonful of pasta salad.

"I had no idea you thought I was." He rather liked the idea she believed that. "Now you know my secret." He grinned. "Eat up. We'll need to blow out the candle to really appreciate what we see."

She took a large bite. "I've lived in cities all my life. Until I came here, I'd never really seen stars without some light. I've heard people talk about them but have never seen them myself. I'm so excited."

With their meal finished, Drake took a few minutes to pack their leftovers away in the bag, leaving the wine out. He blew out the candle and lay back on the blanket with his hand beneath his head and legs stretched out and ankles crossed. "Come join me. This is the best way to see the sky."

Trice lay beside him in the same manner. "Oh, wow. I had no idea the sky could be so big."

"Yeah, this I will miss living in the city," he said softly.

"It's just beautiful." She continued to look up.

He admired Trice. "It's not the only thing."

Trice glanced at him to find him watching her. Her skin heated. She looked back at the sky. A pink wave of light emerged. Then a green one. They appeared to dance with each other. A vivid blue joined them.

"Oh, wow. The aurora borealis. I never thought I would ever see it." She couldn't take her eyes off the show in the sky. "I love it." She would remember this forever. She couldn't believe the colors. The view was everything she ever thought it might be. It went on forever.

She grabbed Drake's hand. "You knew, didn't you? Of course you did."

Drake held her hand. "The lights are a regular this time of year when it is clear."

"They look like they are dancing. Or fabric flowing across a black backdrop. Oh, I know. Like those trapeze artists who wrap themselves in silks and twist and turn."

Drake laughed. "And the list goes on."

"I can't help it. They are amazing."

He couldn't stop grinning. "I love watching you. Hearing you express your pleasure."

"Thank you so much for bringing me here. Next to finding out I might have real family here, this is the best." She wrapped her arms around his neck, kissing him. Just as quickly, she pulled away, and her attention returned to the sky.

He nudged her back to him. "Come lie beside me. Rest your head on my shoulder. Get comfortable."

Trice did what he suggested with a sigh and

snuggled close. He was warm and hard and felt like security. This she could do for the rest of her life. Except they didn't have that long. And she refused to get attached.

They said nothing for a long time.

"Drake, are you asleep?" She placed a hand on his chest.

"No." The word brushed her ear. "I was just enjoying knowing you were beside me, sharing this beautiful sky."

"We didn't have to do this tonight if you were tired." Still, she was glad they came.

His hand ran up and down her arm. "There's not too many more nights left to do it."

He sounded as sad as she felt. "I don't want to think about that."

Drake didn't respond. Had she said the wrong thing? Yet it was the truth. She should've kept the thought to herself. Now that she had said it, she had no choice but to speak. "I will miss you."

In the dark, she felt more than saw him roll toward her. Her heart plummeted.

Drake placed his large hand on her stomach.

Her muscles rippled. Her nerves shot like live wires in response. "It's been fun getting to know you," she said.

"How's your back feeling?"

Even in the poor light, she could tell his face hovered over hers. "It aches a little bit."

With a minimum of movement, he pulled her on top of him. "Is this better?"

"Much."

"Trice, may I kiss you?"

"Why don't I kiss you instead?" Unable to make out his features clearly, she still knew every dip and rise, curve and angle of his face. Her lips found his without searching. As if pulled to them by a string.

His mouth was firm, warm and welcoming. He took. He gave. He suggested. He accepted.

She'd found heaven.

The tip of his tongue ran the width of her lips. She opened for him. Their tongues danced like the colors in the sky. Blending, meeting and swaying to each other and then away. The heat between them built.

His hand moved to her back. She winced.

His head jerked back. "I'm so sorry. I didn't mean to hurt you."

Trice planned to kiss his lips, but her mouth landed on his nose. "I'm fine."

"I just got caught up—" His voice sounded anxious.

"I can't think of anything more flattering. Kiss me again." She leaned down.

His hands came to her shoulders. "Not until I've checked your back. I would never forgive myself if I hurt you."

She sighed and crawled off him. "You're making too much of it."

"Maybe so, but that's the way it's going to be. I'm going to need good light. Do you mind if we go to my place? There are pillows and a big porch with rocking chairs where you can sit in comfort for as long as you like without your back hurting."

She wanted to go with him to his home, to his bed if he wanted her. She wanted to know all there was about Drake, see how he lived, feel his arms around her again. "Okay, my back would appreciate that."

He flipped on a flashlight.

"You think of everything."

"Experience."

She didn't like the idea. "Do you bring women up here often?"

"Why Trice, are you fishing for information about my love life?"

She was confident that his teasing tone was meant to ease her thoughts, but it didn't. She might have been concerned, but she would never admit it. "Dr. Stevansson, don't let your ego get ahead of you."

"To keep the peace, I can say I have never brought another woman to this spot. Now, does that calm your ruffled feathers?"

"My feathers aren't ruffled." They were though. She didn't like the idea of him sharing something as special as the last hour with any-one else.

"It didn't sound that way to me." He returned to putting the wine and glasses away.

She stood out of the way, holding the flashlight as he folded the blanket.

"I'm flattered you wanted to know." He gave her the blanket, then turned his attention to the plastic sheet. "The question you really want the answer to is, do I think you are special?"

"You are so…egotistical." He was making her mad now. Maybe that was the plan. It would put some space between them. She had to remind herself not to let emotions get involved.

He stepped to her, into her personal space. "That may be true, but it's also true that I do think you're special. Very special. I would like to show you how much if you will let me. But no pressure. I'll only go as far as you wish."

Drake pulled up his drive. Trice hadn't said a word since leaving their picnic spot. He wasn't sure if this was a good or bad thing. Worry had started to nag at him. Had he come on too strong? He only had a few more days with Trice and didn't have the time to miss out on a minute of them.

He had left one interior light on, which made the A-frame house glow on the high hill.

"Drake, what a wonderful place. I can imagine the view during the day."

"It's a nice one. You can see almost the entire fjord." One he would miss when he moved away. He drove to the house and around to the back and pulled under a carport. He turned to her. "Still want to come in?"

"Of course I do." Trice grabbed the door handle and got out. She walked round to his side of the truck. "Let me help carry stuff in."

"I've got it. Just the food bag. The blanket and the plastic sheet I'll leave for later."

Drake went ahead of her, flipping on the light switch. He set the bag on the kitchen counter.

Trice entered more slowly. "What a kitchen. I might learn to cook if I had one like this."

"You are welcome to use it anytime." He moved further into the one large room, kicking off his shoes near the sofa. "Come on out to the porch. I'll get you a pillow for your back."

She wandered in his direction as if taking it all in.

"You are thinking mighty hard over there."

"This place is amazing." Trice trailed a finger along his leather sofa.

"I'm glad you like it. Make yourself at home. I'll be right back." Drake soon returned with a pillow. He offered his hand, and Trice took it. After leading her outside to the front porch, he settled her in a rocker with the pillow behind her back. "You enjoy the lights while I get us something hot to drink."

Drake quickly put together hot chocolates from supplies his mother had left behind the last time she had visited. He hadn't had it since he was a child, but he thought Trice might enjoy it. She seemed like that type. He soon returned to her with mugs in hand.

She took hers with a smile on her face. "Hot chocolate. With a marshmallow even." Lifting the mug to her lips, she took a sip. "Perfect."

He sat in the rocker next to hers. "I'm glad you like it."

"Do the lights go on like this all night?" She looked out beyond them.

"They do. They lengthen and get thinner with the season. Then leave to return." Was that what he would do? His grandmother lived here. He would be back, but would Trice be here? She could come and go, but for him it was more complicated.

"With time everything changes." Melancholy hung in her voice.

"It does." Drake didn't want to talk about him leaving. He wanted to live in the here and now. With Trice.

They sat in silence for a while.

Drake liked that. It was rare to find someone he felt comfortable enough to just find pleasure in just being with. "Trice?"

"Mmm?" She sipped her hot chocolate.

"I know the timing is all wrong. I'm going away, and you are staying here. There are only four days left before I leave."

"Are you trying to depress me?"

"No. What I'm trying to say, poorly obviously, is that I don't want to waste what little time we have together by pretending I don't want you in my bed."

Trice looked at him. She stood and offered her hand. "I'm getting cold, and I haven't had a tour of your house yet."

This wasn't going the way he had hoped. After baring his soul, he hadn't expected she'd ask for a tour. He wasn't sure whether to laugh or be insulted.

She walked around him and headed inside.

He picked up the mugs and followed. Trice wasn't in the living room where he thought she would be waiting. He took the dirty dishes to the kitchen sink. "Trice?"

"Up here."

He tracked her voice up the stairs to the loft master bedroom. What was going on?

"Drake? Are you coming?"

He stopped in the bedroom doorway. His heartbeat bumped up three paces. Trice wore one of his dress shirts and stood in the middle of the room. Sexiest sight he'd ever seen. He hoped he wasn't reading this view wrong.

"I thought we could start the tour here. If you don't mind?" Her sweet voice pulled him to her.

He looked at her from head to toe. His gaze captured hers, held as he deliberately walked her direction. "You better not be teasing me, Trice."

A Mona Lisa smile graced her lips. She placed a hand on his chest over his heart. "I would never tease about something so important."

Drake's anticipation went up. Being with him was important to her. One of his hands went to the hem of his shirt, his fingertips brushing the smooth skin of her outer thigh.

Trice's intake of breath told him she was as aware of the sexual tension in the room as he was. Yet she didn't move. Instead, her expression dared him. "I don't think my shirt ever looked this good on me."

She stepped back a couple of paces. "This old thing?"

He moved toward her. "That happens to be my newest shirt."

"That must be why it was hanging on the closet door." She took another step back.

"I was planning to pack it." He moved forward.

That took some of the light out of her eyes. "Let's not talk about that."

"Agreed. What would you like to talk about?"

"I'd rather you kiss me. I like your kisses."

Drake reached for her. His mouth found hers. Trice's arms circled his neck. His hands at her waist pulled her to him. She used her fingers on his shoulders to come up on her toes to reach his lips.

This time he made sure his hands stayed on her hips, not touching her back. Trice didn't make him request she open her mouth. She invited and welcomed him. He might combust right then if he wasn't careful. She never stopped surprising him.

Trice ran her fingers through the hair at the nape of his neck, urging him to deepen the kiss. He didn't disappoint her. His tongue twirled with hers. She pressed against him. His manhood throbbed with desire.

His hand slid over her hip to her thigh. He ran his palm along it, then up and down again to return. The last time he stopped at the elastic of her panties. His index finger nudged under the panty line.

Trice moaned and shifted her hips, her lips placing kisses along his jaw.

His finger moved lower toward the junction of her legs. Heat dwelled there. She shifted, opening her legs. An encouragement. One he didn't need but appreciated. He retreated. This time her moan was more of a complaint.

"Patience, my eager lovely." He went down on a knee and reached under her shirt until he found the top of her panties.

Trice's hands came to rest on his shoulders for support. He slowly removed the material as if revealing a present at Christmas. A perfect present. One he had asked for.

She shimmied and the panties fell to her feet. He had to focus on a spot beyond her for fear he might explode right then. Trice had him thinking and acting like a man starved for a woman. He was. For her. Hooking the tiny piece of clothing on her foot, she lifted it and flung it across the room.

He captured a thigh with a hand.

"Drake." His name was nothing more than a whisper.

He kissed the inside of her thigh. "Sweet."

Trice quivered. Her fingers brushed the hair at the top of his head.

"Liked that, did you?"

She tugged on his hair.

He stood. Her lips found his. Her hands went under his shirt and lifted it. He stepped back and scooped it off, letting it drop to the floor. Trice's palms rested on his pectorals. She ran her hands up and along his shoulders. He remained still, soaking in the pleasure of her touch. His hands rested on her hips. He was ever mindful of her back.

"This is nice," she murmured across his chest before she kissed him just below his neck.

His lips found hers. Tasted and absorbed the brilliance of her. The feel of her against him.

Drake wanted this to go on forever. He paused. But it couldn't.

Trice studied him a moment. "Everything okay? Did I do something wrong? You want me to go?"

She acted so secure, yet with the slightest suggestion she might not be wanted, she over-compensated. He forgot how vulnerable her back-ground made her. "Sweetheart, if you left now, I would have to follow you."

A soft smile formed on her lips. "Would you?"

"All the way to your front door, begging you to come back."

She grinned. "I like the idea of seeing the whole town watching you."

His gaze fixed on hers. "I'm not ashamed of everyone knowing I'm crazy about you."

Trice's smile grew wider. "I'm crazy about you too. Please kiss me again. I like it when you kiss me."

He cupped her face. His lips touched hers, wanting her to know he meant everything he had said. Her arms came around him, and she hugged him as if he were her lifeline. Her hands roamed his chest, then his back. He loved being in her arms. Couldn't get enough of it. Drake wanted to trace her smooth, hot skin once more. Run-ning his hands down her neck, over the ridge of her shoulders, he then moved them to her waist. There he gathered the shirt until his fingers found what he searched for. His hands traveled over the spheres of her butt, pulling her to him, raising her to her toes.

She brushed her center against his solid length. It strained, held in check by his jeans. He lowered her along him. She kissed his neck, then nibbled at the same spot. Holding her with a hand at the waist, he eased his other hand to her center. Wet heat waited for him. Heated his blood. Thrilled him.

Trice's breath caught. She widened her stance, giving clear access. He accepted it. Slipping his finger inside, he felt her tighten around him. She stilled, gripping his shoulders. He pulled his finger from her and entered again.

Trice leaned against him. He held her low on the waist, still aware of her injury. She lowered against his finger and rose again. He gave her what she wanted, pushed upward.

Finding her small nub, he teased her with the tip of his finger. She tensed and groaned, wiggling against his manipulations. After three quick inhales, she ground out, "Drake, please."

Picking up the speed of the movement of his finger, he held her pressed against him. With a sound of joy, she plummeted over the edge to her release.

Drake grinned when her knees buckled and

she went limp against him. He swept her into his arms and carried her to the bed. Laying her carefully on it, he came down beside her.

# CHAPTER EIGHT

TRICE BASKED IN the gratification of Drake's love-making. She lay on the bed with her eyes closed, regaining her breath and composure. Her dazed look met Drake's. A grin rode his lips. The man was pleased with himself. He should be.

She reached for him. He came to her. "It's time I return the favor."

"That sounds nice."

"Lie back." He did. She kissed him. Her hands roamed his chest and stopped to remove his belt. She released it and tugged it from the belt loops, dropping it to the floor.

"Let me help." Drake sat up beside her, then quickly removed his socks before standing to take off the rest of his clothes. They were dropped to the floor.

She watched with appreciation. His body was well taken care of. Drake stood in front of her in all his bare splendor, then came down beside her. Trice sucked in a breath. She'd seen many male bodies, but none were as magnificent as Drake's.

The thought that he wanted her humbled Trice. He looked into her eyes as if he really saw her.

Trice shifted. "You are staring. You're starting to embarrass me."

Drake cupped her cheek. "I was just marking you in my memory, thinking how beautiful you look." His finger drifted away from her face to travel along her neck to the first button of the shirt. He flipped it open.

Trice's breath came faster with every movement of his fingers. She squirmed.

"Please don't move." His focus shifted lower. With each empty buttonhole, the shirt revealed more of her to his view. Drake's eyes burned bright with desire, which fueled her own.

Drake stopped the descent just below her belly button. He ran the back of his hand slowly back up, ending between her breasts. Using only a finger, he pushed the shirt away enough to reveal a breast.

Her center throbbed as Drake lowered his mouth to cover her nipple. Heat flooded her. Her breath came in jerks. Could she stand much more of this? Could she live without it?

Drake nudged her gently to her back, shifting the shirt to reveal both her breasts. His mouth moved to her other breast. Could anything feel so wonderful as having Drake's lips on her? Her fingers played in his hair as he teased and lavished attention on her nipples.

His hand rested on her middle. He found the last two buttons on the shirt and released them, leaving her completely exposed.

"You're so amazing." Drake kissed her belly button. His mouth whispered over her skin until his lips found hers. His hand dipped lower to tease her center.

Two could play that game. Trice's hand wrapped his solid length.

Drake stilled. A moment later, he removed her hand. He looked at her. "Trice, I want you and can't wait any longer to have you. Say you want me too."

"I want you."

Drake rolled away and pulled out the bedside table drawer. He removed a square package, covered himself and turned to her. Reaching beyond her, he placed a pillow beside her. "I don't want to be responsible for hurting you further. Let's put the pillow behind your back."

"I have a better idea." She tugged on his hand. "You lie down."

He did. She straddled him. Drake's eyes widened a second before a wicked gleam entered them. She leaned down to kiss him, her hair creating a curtain. His hands found her waist and skimmed upward until he held a breast in each hand.

Trice lifted on her knees, bringing her center over the tip of his manhood. Slowly she lowered herself down on him. With a sharp lift of his hips, she captured all of him. She moved in a steady up-and-down motion.

She looked at Drake. His eyes were closed, and his face was twisted in a look of unspoiled pleasure. Suddenly he flipped her, braced on his hands he rose over her and reentered with gentleness. Even during his fierce desire, he showed concerned for her injury. He plunged full-hilt and sent her spiraling into the clouds. She hung there, absorbing the bliss and slowly floating back to reality.

Drake's look locked with hers. He retreated and returned, as he drove toward his release. He groaned her name long and reverently before he fell to the bed beside her. With his breathing still deep and quick, he pulled her close and kissed the top of her ear.

Trice smiled and placed her hand over his resting on her stomach.

Drake woke in a panic in the middle of the night. He was in trouble. Big trouble. Like nothing he had ever known. Worse than the fifth grade when he had two girlfriends at the same time. He cared for Trice, far more than he should. This time he couldn't just break up with her and move on. Trice wouldn't be easily pushed away or dismissed.

He had plans. Plans he needed to keep. Important plans. But he couldn't have it both ways. Trice wanted what he was leaving. More than that, he needed to use his skills. He needed to finish his training. That would never happen in Seydisfjordur. There just wasn't the population to give him enough experience.

Could he ask her to come with him? Would she? Did she care for him enough to do that?

"Hey," Trice said from where she slept curled against his side. "Something wrong?"

"Nothing." And everything. "Except I'm not making love to you."

Her hand ran across his chest and back, caressing him, encouraging. "You can remedy that, Doc."

He rolled toward her. "You think I'm just the medicine you need."

She kissed him. "I know you are."

He groaned when she ran a finger along his already hardening manhood. "You keep that up and I'll be the answer to all your problems."

Her look turned sassy. "Who says you aren't already?"

Drake wished he was. He feared he had created more problems, but he couldn't have stop himself. Trice made his heart swell and his body hum. "Back okay?"

"I'll be fine. Just kiss me."

He would take the here and now and worry about later—later.

\* \* \*

That morning, he slipped out of bed, leaving a soft, warm Trice behind. Maybe if he went into another room, he could think clearer. Figure out how to complete his surgery training and have Trice at the same time.

In the kitchen he prepared a light breakfast. He had his head straightened out by then. His determination was back in place. He would be leaving in a few days. He had his spot waiting on him in London. If he didn't take it, then it might be years before he had another chance. Trice would be a wonderful memory. With that decided, he would make the most of the time he had with her.

He jerked to a stop in the doorway. She still lay facedown on his sheets. The sun streaming across Trice's bare skin made it glow. The sight had him filing it away in his memory.

Drake recognized the moment Trice woke. She stretched like a feline, coming up on her hands and lifting her behind in the air, and then bringing her abdomen to the sheets again. His manhood shot to ready in seconds, watching her erotic movements. His flannel sleep pants did little to cover his reaction. The tray in his hand shook. He carried it with the steaming mugs of coffee, boiled eggs and toast to the bedside table. "Good morning, sleepyhead. I was starting to think you were never going to wake."

"Good morning. What have you been up to?"

"I thought you might like something to eat." He placed the tray on the bedside table before he dropped it.

"You are always so considerate." Her hand brushed his arm from elbow to wrist. "Where's my...uh...your shirt?"

"Don't feel like you need to put something on for me." Drake found the shirt and handed it to her.

She turned her back to him, slipping her arms in the sleeves, then buttoning it. "What time is it?"

Disappointment filled him, but it was probably just as well. He needed the distraction. "It's still early."

"We should be at the clinic on time since we were gone a day and a half. I still have to prove myself. I want the town to know I'll be there for them."

Unlike what he would be for his grandmother. Still, she was the one pushing him to go. Trice would be here. She would be here to see to Luce. But it was his responsibility. He had to move past this. Up until ten days ago, he'd had it all settled in his mind. Now uncertainly had creeped in. Slowly Trice had become the center of his world. That had to end.

Trice raised her arms in the air for another big stretch. She looked at the tray. "What do you have here?"

"Our breakfast." He picked up the tray and set it in the center of the bed.

"Looks good. We'll get food all over your sheets." She picked up a napkin.

"Like I care about that."

She grinned. "You might not until you wake with crumbs all over you." She took a bite of toast, making sure to keep it over the tray.

Drake enjoyed a nice view of her breasts in the gaping shirt.

She looked toward the window. "This I could get used to, waking up to this green valley with the ice blue of the fjord surrounded by the snow-tipped mountains. I can imagine watching a storm coming is magnificent."

He knew all the views well. But he must give those and other things up to reach his goal. "Almost as magnificent as the view I have now."

Trice followed the direction on his look. She sat straighter. "I don't see how you can leave this house either. Are you going to sell it?"

"No. My family will come here for holidays and visits. My parents built this house. For the view. I bought it when they moved." He took a bite out of a boiled egg.

She added butter to her bread. "I've seen nothing in the village like it."

"No, all the materials had to be shipped in. It took a couple years before we could move in. Everyone said Dad was crazy to put all the glass in the house since it's so cold here, but my parents wanted to feel like a part of nature. They felt like the view was worth it. There is special wire in the glass to warm it. They also added special insulation and thick drapes that disappear into a wall pocket that are used for heat and light control on the long days."

Trice shook her head. "I don't see how you can leave it."

"You're not making this any easier."

"I'm sorry. That isn't my intent." She took a sip of coffee looking at him over the rim. "Do you think you will have a chance today to call Mr. Bjonsson?"

"For you I will make a point to. I'd like to be the one to introduce you."

She put her mug down on the tray. "I better get dressed so you can take me home to get changed." She moved to get off the bed.

"Before you do that, let me check your back." He went to her side of the bed.

"You're still worried about my back?"

"I hope I didn't make it worse."

She looked directly at him. "It is fine. If it weren't, it would have been worth it."

"I'll take that as a compliment." He grinned. "You'll have to take the shirt off."

She looked over her shoulder with a teasing grin. "Are you sure you're not just doing this to get me to undressed?"

"I can't deny the idea has appeal. But I actually want to have a look at your back." He moved the tray back to the bedside table.

"You didn't hurt me, I promise." She lowered the shirt over her shoulders while looking back at him.

"Quit arguing. I would like to see for myself." He kissed her shoulder and down her back. "I think you'll recover nicely." He reached around her to cup her breasts.

She leaned against him. Her warmth met his heat. "How much time do we have?"

He turned her to face him. "Enough."

Trice watched Drake put the last stitch in the nine-year-old boy's head. The child had fallen and busted his head open. Drake had great surgery skills. He hadn't hesitated about handling the emergency. He had swiftly and confidently prepared the area while at the same time putting the boy and his mother at ease.

As much as Trice hated to see him leave, she understood he had commitments he must honor. His skills were too great for a small clinic that would see little need. Still, she dreaded the time she had to watch him go. She had made a deal with herself not to think about how many days Drake had left. Her plan was to make the most out of the time they had together.

She had to remain strong and detached if she wanted to survive.

That morning after breakfast, they had made love in the sunshine. Never had she been quite as free or bold in her lovemaking, confident in her body. She spent most of her life insecure in her personal relationships because she had had so few, but with Drake she had opened up and given her all. He had given her that security and confidence. For that she would always be grateful.

The next man in her life would have a lot to live up to after Drake. As if by a silent mutual agreement, they had decided not to discuss him leaving, as if they were going to pretend he would always be there.

She stood there and watched Drake tie off the last stitch and snip off the thread like a lovesick teen. Love? Was she in love with him? She had only known him a little over a week. She couldn't be. Love took longer than that to develop. Yet the moments they had shared had been more intense than any she had ever felt.

The bell ringing on the door of the clinic refocused her attention. She stepped out of the exam room and walked down the short hall to the front. "Can I help you?"

"We are here to see Dr. Stevansson." A middle-aged woman stood there with a preteen girl beside her.

"I'll be taking over for Dr. Stevansson." Trice didn't like the taste of those words on her tongue. She wished Drake would be here tomorrow, the next day and all those that would fellow. "I'm Dr. Shell."

"You're the woman who saved those two men's lives," the preteen stated.

"That was more of a team effort." Trice looked between the woman and the girl. "Now, what can I do for you?"

The woman lifted her foot. "I have foot pain. I thought it was getting better, but this morning I could hardly stand."

"Come back this way." Trice turned toward the examination room.

The woman hobbled across the floor, supported by the girl.

Trice pointed to the examination room. "Please have a seat in the chair. What's your name?"

"Maude Traustason. This is my daughter, Lula."

The girl stood beside the woman.

"Nice to meet you both. Well, Maude, can you tell me what's going on with your foot?" Trice pulled the stool forward and took a seat.

"Drake says I have plantar fasciitis. He told me to soak it, but I don't have time. I have to work at the cannery and take care of my kids. Is there something else I can do?"

"Please take your shoe and sock off and let me have a look." While the woman removed them, Trice continued, "Do you stand on cement all day? Or sit at a desk?"

"I walk on cement most of the time." The woman dropped a shoe to the floor.

"Have you been taking an anti-inflammatory?" She peeled off her sock. "I did for a while."

"Did it help?" Trice looked at the woman.

"It did."

"May I see your foot?" Trice rolled the stool closer and placed the lifted heel across her legs. The red angry skin made her flinch. It had to hurt. "I'm going to touch it." She looked at Maude. "Please don't kick me."

"It really hurts." Maude's face twisted up.

"I don't doubt it." Trice examined the foot with a gentle hand, then lowered it to the floor. She picked up the woman's shoe. "Is this what you wear to work?"

"Yes."

"Then I would suggest you get a pair with more support. Especially in the heel area. Did Dr. Stevansson give you some exercises to do?"

"He did."

"Good. Be creative about when you do them. At work when you have a moment, do just one or two at a time. At night I want you to soak your feet. Others will have to help—" she looked at the girl "—or you'll just have to let something go, or this won't get better. I also want you to take an anti-inflammatory on the days you work, and come back to see me if you aren't better in two weeks. I can't stress enough that soaking your feet is important."

The woman nodded. "Okay."

"And you really should buy some better shoes."

"All right."

She glanced at Drake standing at the door. He had been listening. She felt him come up a few minutes earlier. Her body had a way of knowing he was around. He had a way of muddling her mind as well. She needed to concentrate on what she was there for and not Drake.

Trice placed Maude's foot on the floor. "May I ask you a medical history question?"

"Okay." Maude looked at her.

"Do you or any of the members of your family have HEP? I'm doing a research project on HEP and would like to interview anyone who has it."

Maude looked at her, not saying anything for a moment, as if deciding if she would offer any help. "I carry the gene. My sister does too."

Trice worked at containing her joy. "Would you be willing to answer a list of questions and allow me to view your medical records?"

Maude appeared unsure but said, "I guess so."

"I'll let you put on your sock and shoe while I go get the questions." Trice hurried toward the door.

Drake stepped out of the doorway to let her pass.

She returned with her electronic pad. Drake

ended his conversation with Maude's daughter and left the room. Trice handed the pad to Maude. "Here, if you would answer these, it would be wonderful. Do you mind if I take Lula for a soda while you're working?"

"That's fine." The woman went to work on the questions.

Trice led Lula toward the back of the building. "I know where Dr. Stevansson hides his soda."

They went to the kitchen area. Trice handed the girl a can of drink. In a falsetto high voice she said, "Don't tell Dr. Stevansson. It's our secret."

"What's going on in here?" Drake popped out from behind the doorframe.

Trice and Lula jumped.

"Caught you. Are you in my snacks again?" He looked from one to the other, then grinned. "Help yourself." He looked directly at Trice. "Since you already have."

"Lula, let's go see if your mother is finished." Trice ushered the girl out of the room as if they had gotten away with a crime.

Lula laughed.

Her mother handed the electronic pad to Trice when they entered. "All done."

Trice took the pad. "Thanks so much, Maude. I really appreciate it. Would you mind letting your sister know about my research and ask her if she would participate?"

Maude's lips thinned. "She doesn't come to town often."

"Do you happen to know any other people who might have the syndrome?" Trice needed to move forward with her project.

"I can ask at my knitting circle tonight. Maybe somebody there does or knows of somebody who does." Maude stood to leave.

Lula headed out the door with soda in hand.

"I would appreciate that." Trice smiled. "Come by and let me know how your foot is doing."

Maude stopped at the door. "Do you knit?"

Trice shook her head. "No, but I've always wanted to learn."

"Why don't you come to our circle tonight? You can meet everyone and give it a try."

Trice looked at Drake, who leaned against the doorframe, talking to Lula. She had planned to spend the evening with him.

He gave her a smile that didn't reach his eyes. "You should go. You will have fun."

She wasn't sure if she was disappointed he didn't discourage her or glad he was unselfish enough not to say anything. She needed to move beyond him anyway. What they had now wouldn't last. She had her future to consider.

Trice's attention returned to Maude. "Thanks. I'd love to come."

Maude smiled. "Good. We meet at Unndis Hanson's house. See you there."

"I don't have any supplies." Where would she find needles and yarn on such short notice?

Drake volunteered, "My mom left some of hers. They're at the house. I'll get them for you."

Trice could have kissed him. "Thanks, Drake. That would be nice."

Maude moved toward the door. "I'll call my sister on my way home. Thanks for your help."

"Come back if the foot doesn't get better. I'll be here to help." Trice saw her out the door. "I look forward to seeing you this evening."

Drake wanted to disagree with the evening plans, but he had no right. Trice needed to become a part of the community, find her own way, one that didn't involve him. He had made the choice to leave town. He shouldn't, wouldn't hold her back. Asking her to forgo the knitting group to spend time with him would be selfish. Her research was important to Trice, and more than, that it was important to people who had the disease. Yet he wanted Trice with him as much as possible.

After Maude and Lula had left, Trice kissed him, her eyes bright. "I am making progress. I'm so excited."

"I never doubted you. I think you can do anything you put your mind to."

She wrapped her hands around his bicep and

pressed against him. "You're just being nice because you like me."

"True." He gave her an indulgent look.

"I'm going to clean up the examination room, then log in Maude's answers and get ready for tonight."

Trice sound so happy, he couldn't bring himself to complain about the plans. "I have some paperwork to do as well if I don't want to stay late tonight. I better get busy."

She gave him a searching look. "You're not angry, are you, about me going to the knitting meeting instead of spending the time with you?"

"No, no. You need to go to the knitting meeting. I understand that."

"I hope so. My research is really important to me. And I want to fit in here."

"I know." He did. What he'd taken for granted all these years, she desperately craved. "You should go."

She kissed him again. "I'm glad you understand."

He pulled her close. "I would understand better with another kiss."

For the next hour, they worked without interruption. Then Drake knocked on the office door where Trice worked. "How about having lunch with me?"

She looked up. "Shouldn't one of us be here?"

"I'll put a note on the door about where we are."

"Okay then." Trice stood.

Before they went out the door, he pulled her into his arms and kissed her. She wrapped her arms around his waist and returned his kiss.

Drake pulled away, looking into her eyes. "Let's forget lunch and lock the door."

Trice giggled, which only made him want to really do what he'd suggested.

She pulled away from him. "That wouldn't do much to instill faith in me. I need to make a good impression on the town."

"I believe you have that covered already." She'd proved her abilities more than once. Luce would be in good hands.

"I can't take any chances on messing that up. And I fear once I get started kissing you, I won't stop."

"Mmm. I like that idea." He gave her another quick but heated kiss.

She placed her hands on his chest. "We better have some lunch and stay out of trouble."

He opened the door. "It's too late for that."

Trice grinned, her look warm. "Maybe."

They headed down the street. Drake was tempted to take her hand but resisted doing so. He didn't know if Trice would appreciate everyone knowing something was happening between them. He was confident that if anyone saw him looking at Trice, they would know right away he was crazy about her.

"Where are we going?"

He pointed down the street. "To the diner for a sandwich."

"We could go to my place. I'll fix you a sandwich." Her eyes held a mischievous light.

"Dr. Shell, are you trying to lure me into bed in the middle of the day?"

"I was just trying to offer you lunch. No agenda." She stopped and fixed him with a twinkling look. "Unlike you, who had me come look at the stars, then lured me to your house to take advantage of me."

His look locked with hers. "I lured you? If I remember correctly, it was you waiting in my bedroom."

Her face pinked sweetly. "I hope I wasn't too bold."

Heat from the memory covered his body. "I couldn't have asked for a nicer welcome."

They continued walking. At the café, he held the door open. The noisy place went quiet. Everyone stopped what they were doing and clapped.

Trice looked at him, perplexed.

He said just for her ears, "They appreciated your work the other day. Come on, let's find a table." He directed her to one in a back corner. Trice took a chair on one side, and he took a chair on the other. He would have liked to have sat next to her, but that would have made his feelings too obvious.

A waitress came from the bar to take their order.

"I'm really looking forward to learning to knit. I'm amazed at all the community activities the town has." Trice was almost buzzing with excitement.

"In the dead of winter, we have to make our own entertainment. We have something almost nightly. In the nice months, we still like to get together. We especially enjoy our folk dancing and singing."

Trice sat forward. "You sing? I know you can dance."

"It's folk dancing. And yes, I do both well enough." He would miss that comradery when he moved to the large city.

"I'd like to hear you sing."

The eagerness in her eyes made him smile. "Maybe I'll sing for you sometime." He looked around, "But it won't be in the middle of lunch."

"And I had so hoped…"

He laughed. "Trice, I think you could get me in trouble."

"Maybe you could teach me a folk dance."

He was impressed with her efforts to acclimatize to the town. He wasn't sure someone else would make the effort. He shouldn't have been surprised. She gave all of herself, and people responded to that. She certainly had to him last night. Like no one else ever had. His greatest fear was that he might not find someone who would ever give so freely again.

How could somebody possibly not want her in their life? He wanted her badly. The problem was, he had made plans that didn't include her. If he did stay, having Trice beside him would make it easier.

The waitress brought their meals, stopping his out-of-control thoughts.

"I meant to tell you on the way over here that I called Bjonsson."

She sat forward. "You did?"

"I didn't get to talk to him, but I left him a message with a woman who answered. She told me she would see to it that he got my message. I will try again before I leave, maybe drive up there."

"Hopefully he will contact you. I won't give up. I'll keep trying even after you are gone."

"I never doubted you would for a minute." He put his sandwich down. "Tomorrow night the town is throwing me a going-away party. Would you like to come?"

The light went out of her eyes. She raised her chin. "I've already been invited. Luce said something about it a few days ago."

"I should've known. It's hard to get ahead of her. Are you planning to come?"

She shook her head. "I don't think so."

He met Trice's eyes. "I'd like for you to be there."

Trice said nothing for a long minute. "I will come if you really want me there."

He moved his legs so hers fit between them and gave them a gentle squeeze.

"You know," she said, "I'm starting to have a very busy social life. I may get busy at the last minute."

"My party is going to be the event of the year, so I don't think I need to worry." At least her good humor had returned.

"It will be another good opportunity for me to meet people."

"I agree. And I promise to help you in that area." He leaned forward so only she would hear him. "Now, how do you plan to repay me?"

She put a finger to her chin as if considering. "I haven't thought about it."

He leaned forward. "Maybe an early thank-you?"

"Like?" She acted innocent.

"I was thinking I could come by after the knitting meeting." Dared he hope she would agree?

"It'll be kind of late."

He crossed his arms and laid them on the table, putting him that much closer to her. "Are you trying to get rid of me already?" He was half teasing and half serious.

"No, I'm trying to figure out how to live without you."

Those words were like a punch in the chest. He hadn't meant to hurt her. Had tried not to. Luce had been right. He should have stayed away.

"I've been thinking maybe we shouldn't see each other again. I'll be alone in a couple nights anyway." Her eyes remained downcast.

"I'm sorry. I just made this assumption that we would see each other every night until I left. My apologies. I shouldn't have done that. I know this isn't easy for you."

"I should be used to it. It has happened enough in my life."

"It wasn't my intention to hurt you." His hand covered hers. He no longer cared what others saw or thought. Trice was hurting because of him.

Trice pulled her hand away and put a smile on her face. "Enough of this. I knew the score when I arrived. After all, I came here to take your place." She shook her head. "Let's enjoy what time we have and not talk about the future."

They both returned to their meal.

He gave a curt nod. Despite the pleasant conversation he tried to participate in, the food in his stomach had soured.

# CHAPTER NINE

AFTER THEIR LUNCH, she and Drake strolled back to the clinic. There he left her to oversee the clinic while working on her research. He drove home, returning with a cloth bag containing two knitting needles and a skein of navy yarn.

"This is wonderful. Thank you so much. Are you sure your mother won't mind?"

"Positive. Now you're all set for this evening."

She wished his support reached his eyes. "I have to say I'm looking forward to it."

"Mind if I walk you to the Hansons' later?" He looked like a puppy left behind.

Trice had to give him something. "Oh, course not."

That brightened his face. She would miss him tonight. Still, she didn't enjoy being a foregone conclusion for the next few nights. Maybe it was just as well they let things stay at a one-night event. Still, she hated seeing Drake look disappointed. "I'm actually nervous about this. I've never had a chance to socialize with a bunch of women. What if they don't like me?"

He roared with laughter. "Like that's going to happen. Everyone you meet likes you."

At the knock on her door, she opened it to Drake. She grabbed her sweater and the knitting bag and stepped outside.

He grinned. "You are excited about this evening."

"I am." She headed toward the street.

His hand on her arm stopped her. "Hold on a minute. I have something I need to do."

Drake's gaze held hers before his face came down to hers. The kiss was sweet, tender. Unlike any other kiss they had shared. With this one, he was trying to tell her something. Did she dare believe he really cared?

He pulled away and rested his forehead against hers. Her breathing had increased. She placed a hand over his heart. The rapid thump there matched hers. "Luce is going to be watching."

"I have no doubt. Luce knows exactly what we've been doing. She knows everything. She'll have something to say about it. She has already gotten on to me."

"For what?"

"She told me not to hurt you."

Trice straightened. "I'm tougher than that."

"I wish I could say the same."

She studied him a moment. "What do you mean by that?"

He met her look. "I'm going to miss you, Beatrice Shell. A lot."

"I will miss you too." She hurt at the thought.

"Maybe our paths will cross again one day."

Many families and temporary friends had said the same to her over the years. None of them had she ever seen again. People got busy. They didn't care enough. She was just forgotten. "Let's enjoy knowing each other now." She stepped out of his reach. "I need to go. I don't want to be late."

A few minutes' walk later, she hesitated at the Hansons' front door.

Drake's hand on her waist was warm and reassuring. He gave her a nudge. "Go on. They will love you. You will have a good time. I'll see you in the morning."

She wanted to turn and walk away with him, but she didn't. Drake didn't even look back to see if she had gone inside. If he had, she would have run to him. Bracing herself, she knocked on the door.

A woman opened the door and invited her in. The living area was bright. Women stood around in groups talking. She moved further into the room without anyone making eye contact or speaking. Worry started to creep in.

Some people could be reserved about talking to anyone new. Trice understood that well. She had hoped tonight would be different. A moment later, Maude hurried toward her.

"Come sit beside me." Maude returned to a chair across the room. "I see you brought something to work with. Good."

The other women in the room moved to their chairs as well.

Trice waited, watching the other women remove their needles and yarn. As if in unison, they began moving their needles, creating a click-click sound while looping yarn. Moments later, they were in conversation about someone she didn't know.

Maude said, "Let me show you."

Trice removed her materials.

Maude said, "Take the needles and hold them in your fingers like this. Attach the yarn."

Trice followed the instructions the best she could. After a couple of false starts, she managed the basics. Soon she had created a row of stitches.

"Now you have to go back the other way."

Trice almost groaned, but she made the effort. Minutes later, she had another row, but with a number of uneven loops. Still, she was proud of her efforts.

While knitting, she listened to the conversations about who was pregnant, who was sick and who would be marrying soon. These were all parts of life within a community. People she would be caring for over the next year, the baby she would help deliver. Her eyes watered. This was part of belonging. A life she had never known. But might have found.

"Dr. Shell, did you really climb down and save two men?" one of the younger women asked.

Trice laid her knitting in her lap. She wouldn't be able to concentrate and talk at the same time. There had been medical problems to solve that had been less frustrating than figuring out how to make identical loops. "I wouldn't exactly put it that way, but yeah. I was the one who climbed down, only because I was the smallest. I could fit in the crevice. And please call me Trice."

She had the entire room's attention. Someone said, "That must've been scary."

Another lady said, "I couldn't have done it."

Trice gave them an indulgent smile. "It was scary more after the fact than at the time. I just did what needed to be done."

"That's pretty impressive," someone else said.

The entire time, their needles never stopped.

Trice cleared her throat, hoping it wasn't too early for this conversation. "As I'm sure you know, I'm taking Dr. Stevansson's place for the next year. While I'm doing that, I will also be doing some research work." This was her chance to say something about HEP. "My research is studying HEP."

The blank faces of the women told her more

explanation would be needed. Trice took a moment to explain the disorder. A number of the women nodded, now understanding what she was referring to.

Trice leaned forward. "In fact, I could use your help. I need to speak to anyone who has had HEP or is willing to be tested for it. If you have had it or know someone who has been tested for it, I would really appreciate you letting me know. I promise there will be nothing or very little that is painful involved."

The room went quiet. The circle just looked at her, saying nothing. Watching.

Trice broke the silence. "I have it. I learned about it when I became sick. That's when I became interested in the disorder. I want to learn more about the disease. I can do that by talking to people."

Suspicion filled the women's eyes. Maybe Trice should have waited on Drake to say something about it. But he had his own life to worry about. He was packing to leave and tying up business. She couldn't depend on him. He would soon be gone.

A woman shifted in her chair. "I was sick with it as a child, and my daughter as well."

Excitement filled Trice's chest. Maybe this would work. "Will you come to see me one day next week? Bring your daughter as well."

The mother nodded.

"Thank you. That would be wonderful."

Another said, "I think my neighbor had it. I'll tell her to come see you."

"I would appreciate it." Trice couldn't help the thrill going through her. She had made progress. Picking up her knitting again, she tried to get in the groove.

Nobody else said anything for a couple of minutes as they returned to their work. Finally, one of the older women said with a sly grin, "What do you think of Drake? He seems to like you."

Each woman eagerly watched her. Their hands automatically moved the needles, but their looks stayed with her. Trice's body warmed. Her hands shook, causing her to drop a loop. "I think he is a great doctor. I know you will miss him."

"He seems smitten with you," a woman with a toothless grin said.

"We are friends." Trice should have expected this. Prepared herself for it.

A giggle went around the room.

"Maybe she could get him to stay," a woman on the other side of Maude said.

Trice looked at each of the women. "I won't be doing that."

Maude took pity on Trice and asked one of the women a question, moving the attention away from her and Drake. Trice wasn't interested in sharing what was happening between them. It was too new and was going to be too short.

The meeting broke up. Trice packed her knitting carefully away. She would continue to practice. Maybe make something for Drake and send it to him. No. They had agreed their fling would end when he left. That would mean no contact.

Trice stepped out into the dim light, fully expecting to find Drake waiting for her. He wasn't. She couldn't help but be disappointed. He was doing as she'd asked. She started home. This time she wished he hadn't abided by her request.

It didn't take her long to walk past Luce's front door and round the corner toward her own home. Her home. She liked the sound of that. It was a small space, but she'd never had a spot all her own. She had always shared with someone else. All her personal belongs could fill her suitcase, but here she had more. It was a place that needed her and where she could belong.

Trice opened her door to the lone light she'd left on. Again a sense of disappointment went through her. Drake wasn't there. She had to move past this expectation. He would be in a matter of days. She had to learn to do without him.

She went about getting ready for bed, and still there was no knock on the door. Wearing her warm pajamas, she climbed under the covers, then turned off the light. She tossed and turned, thinking of how little time she had to spend with Drake. Worse, she had told him she wouldn't see him personally again. Why had she insisted on doing that? To protect herself.

She was only hurting herself. Early in her life, she had learned not to let anyone close because she would soon leave, but this time she wanted as much of Drake as she could get. They had so little time. She wanted to create more happy memories.

At the tap on her window, she jerked straight up. Another tap. She walked to the window. A face was pressed against it. Drake.

He pointed toward the door.

She hurried to it. "What are you doing here in the middle of the night? Is something wrong?"

He stepped into her personal space, far enough that she stepped back. He kept coming, closing the door behind him. "Yes, there is."

"I'll get dressed."

"I was thinking you need to get undressed."

Trice met his look. His eyes held a predatory gleam. "What are you up to?"

"I came to see you. I missed you. I couldn't sleep." He sounded pitiful.

She liked the idea of him needing her. "Why were you tapping on the window instead of knocking on the door?"

"I was trying to be quiet." He moved toward her again. This time her back came up against the wall. "Luce has ears like a twenty-year-old." His lips brushed hers. His cool hands came to rest under her pajama top at her waist.

She shuddered. "Your hands are freezing."

"How about warming them up?" He nuzzled her neck.

She gave him a light slap on the shoulder. "You're crazy. People are already talking about us."

"So? We're adults." His lips found hers before they traveled down her neck, leaving kisses along the way. "You will let me stay the night, won't you?"

She couldn't resist him. "What kind of doctor would I be if I didn't take care of a man in need of warming?"

"My thoughts exactly." His lips met hers as he brought her against him. He began walking her backwards towards the bed.

Sometime later, Trice lay beside Drake, her head resting on his shoulder and her hand tracing circles on his chest. Why couldn't she have this all the time? Life seemed to always be shoving her out of the way.

"You know, I could do this forever." Drake gave her a gentle squeeze.

"It is nice."

"I wish we had longer. We only have tomorrow night left, and part of that will be taken up with my going-away party." He sounded as if he'd like to forget about the party.

She kissed the side of his jaw. "We agreed not to talk about you leaving."

"I know, but I think we should." He rolled so he could see her face.

"And accomplish what?" She didn't want to go down this road. It was too muddy, sticky.

"I was hoping for a compromise. Will you come visit me? I could come here some." Even he didn't sound confident about how that would work.

Her hand fell away from his chest. "I would like that. But soon it would become difficult for us to get away. Then slowly we would get too busy to see each other at all. We would just be prolonging the inevitable. I've lived it all my life."

Drake's face turned to one of hurt and disappointment. "You don't even want to try?"

"I have tried—before. Everyone says they will stay in touch, but no one does. It's a lot more painful to let things drag on. To hope for a phone call. To look for a letter. To make plans that must be canceled. You need to leave here and embrace your new life. It's what you want. I need to find my place in the world. Let's make the most of the here and now." She brushed her fingertip across his chest.

"You don't have much faith in people, do you? I'm not one of those who will forget you. You don't have to be alone all your life. Have you ever thought it was a two-way street? That you could have tried to stay in contact as well?"

"I was a child—"

"But what about those you went to medical school with? How many of those people have you tried to stay in touch with? Or your last foster mother?"

"I...uh..."

"Exactly. I think we have something worth trying to build on. But both of us have to want it. To work at it. Have faith that we can do it. I know your past tells you that there are no lasting relationships, but I care about you. I won't let you go."

She shook her head.

A deep sadness filled his eyes. "You won't even try, will you?"

"You have an intense year ahead of you. You won't have time to come here. You shouldn't have distractions. I'm not going anywhere at least for a year. I can't just leave anytime I want, and neither will you be able to."

A stream of anger went through Drake. "I have agreements and obligations as well. I've been trying to get back to my surgery training for two years. If I don't go now, I might never get to go. Space may not open up at another time. What I learn could make the difference in someone's life. Even my grandmother's. She isn't getting any younger. Now is my chance to get that training."

Trice pushed up on an elbow so their looks met. "I don't blame you. Your skills are needed.

That's how I felt about coming here. It was something I had to do."

"It would be too difficult to get another placement." He needed the training to bring it home to Iceland.

"Hey, I'm not asking you to stay for me. I would never do that no matter how tempted I am to do so. We need to face it. The time just isn't right for us."

He wanted to shake her. "I don't want to accept that. You're too important to me."

She lay beside him again. "You can't accept it because you've never had to live it."

"I'm not one of those who will forget you when I'm gone. You don't give me enough credit."

Trice offered him a wry smile. "I have to go with what I know."

"I can and will prove you wrong. What will you do when you leave here?"

"I don't know. I'll be trying to get my research paper published. Then find a place to practice medicine. If they will have me, I might stay here."

She wanted what he was giving up. Why had he found her now? "Why here?"

"I really like it. I feel at home."

Just as it had been to him. "You wait until you spend a winter here. You might change your mind. I was hoping you might come to London. We could come back to Iceland when the time was right."

"You know that isn't easy for an American."

"Could we at least stay in contact? Online. Write."

She sighed and rolled over on him. "Why don't we concentrate on another form of communication right now?"

He ran his hands gently up her smooth back while she gave him a wet, hot kiss. He must find a way to keep her in his arms.

Trice woke when Drake left her bed early, before daylight, with a sweet kiss that had her reaching to hold him to her. How would she survive when he left? She didn't want to consider it, but that was all she could think about. She wanted to forget about their conversation. It had hurt too much to tell him no. To discourage him. Some of what Drake had said was true. That wasn't what really bothered her. The problem was, she had been left after promises had been made to keep in contact. Too many times that had failed.

All she said was true. In time they would get too busy for each other. Distance would kill what they had. It was easier just to shut it down now. She had never intended for it to get this complicated.

In fact, it should've been only for one night and that's it. They had both known the score going in. The plan had been for their relationship to remain short and sweet. They should have kept it that way, but she couldn't. She wanted Drake too badly. Now she would put it all behind her. Her life had given her plenty of experience in how to do that.

He would be gone in little more than twenty-four hours. After that, she would figure out how to survive. If he managed to return for a visit or they had a chance to see each other, she would make the most of that as well. She had no doubt he would soon find somebody in the big city of London. It wouldn't take much for him to forget her. Of this she was confident.

Drake's surgery training should take priority. He had made it clear what his dream was. That meant he needed to leave Seydisfjordur. She wouldn't be a part of making him unhappy. That she promised herself and him as well.

Not a person to scare easily, she was terrified now. With knowledge of a few relationships, and none of those ending well, she had no doubt she and Drake would end the same way. Yet she dared to dream they could be different. That they might really have something worth fighting for.

He'd been more than a wonderful distraction. This was the first time she'd been in love. Drake's leaving would hurt. Deeply.

Entering the clinic, she found Drake in the storage room with his iPad in hand. "Hey."

His face lit up. He set his pad down and wrapped his arms around her. His lips found hers.

She clung to him. He kissed her breathless. Her knees had gone weak by the time he let her go. "Will you come to my house after the party tonight? I still have that book to give you."

"How could I say no after that kiss? And I do want to read that book."

He grinned. "You are going to miss me."

Heaven help her, she was.

The rest of the day, she vacillated between walking on air and deep depression. She could hardly concentrate on her patients. To her great delight, two people came in to help with her research.

"You must have won them over last night," Drake commented after a man left.

Trice sat in the office. "I don't know about that."

"I've never known them to open up to a stranger like they have you. But you do have a way of bringing that out in people." He sounded proud of her, and she liked that idea.

"I wouldn't have thought that. It hasn't happened before." How many homes had she been in where she'd just blended into the background? They had decided she wasn't a good fit for them. In Seydisfjordur, she seemed to have blossomed.

"Will you be going back to the knitting circle?" He continued to lean against the doorframe.

"I think I will. I started a project, and I would like to try to finish it." She would return to the circle if for no other reason than being part of the group.

"And what is your project?"

She grinned "I hope it's the beginning of a hat."

"I'm impressed. I look forward to seeing it finished."

A hush filled the air. They both knew that wouldn't happen.

Trice quickly tried to cover up the heavy moment. "My knitting leaves a lot to be desired. I just have never been asked to be a part of something."

His brows rose. "Never? How could somebody not notice you are amazing?"

"Maybe a study group, but come to think of it, I asked them. It doesn't matter. It's just nice to have a place to belong."

Drake placed his arm around her shoulders, held her tight and kissed her temple. "Seydisfjordur is lucky they have you."

What had she done to deserve Drake? She was in trouble.

# CHAPTER TEN

IT HAD BEEN a long time since Drake had been nervous before any event, especially one taking place in his hometown. Yet here he was, getting ready to face his family and friends, and tonight his hands were damp.

He couldn't believe he was this close to getting what he'd been dreaming of for so long. But the gloss was off because of Trice. How was he going to leave her? Her hand holding his bicep only reminded him of how much he wanted her close.

Drake opened the door to the community center. The group gathered must have been the entire town and surrounding area. The clapping started and continued to the point that he hung his head and shook it with embarrassment.

Trice moved off to the side, leaving him standing in the middle of a horseshoe of smiling people.

The longer he looked into the smiling faces of people he'd known all his life, the more overwhelmed he became.

The mayor stepped forward and commanded everyone's attention. It took a moment for the noise to die down. "We're going to have our meal and then the program."

Program? He hadn't expected that. The meal, yes, but that was all. He looked at Trice to see if she knew anything about that.

She pursed her lips and shrugged her shoulders. He wasn't getting any help there. Then Trice's mouth formed a smile. She apparently liked seeing him unsure. His grandmother proved even less help.

The mayor said to him, "Now, you and the new doctor go first. We have a place for you right up front at the main table."

He and Trice moved to the table that had so much food on it, he feared he heard it groan. He asked into Trice's ear, "Do you know what's going on?"

Over her shoulder, she said sweetly, "I have no idea. I believe most of this must've been planned a long time before I came. Here you had me believing you were a man who had his ear to the ground and knew everything going on in town."

The smile left his face. "Apparently not. Because I haven't heard a word about this."

"Just sit back and enjoy it. They're only showing you how valuable you have been to the community."

Why hadn't he put more value on that? He'd

certainly known it where Dr. Johannsson had been concerned. He just had never thought of himself in the same terms.

Trice went about filling her plate. She stopped and looked at him. "Are you okay?"

"Yeah, yeah, I'm fine."

With food in hand, they were directed to the front table.

Trice hesitated. "I shouldn't be seated up here."

"You're with me. My guest sits beside me." He needed her there.

People began filling the other tables. A number of them approached him to share how much they had appreciated him. Helga Olafsdottir told him thanks for taking care of her broken arm. Einar Abelsson said thanks for stitching up his hand. Lydia Einarsson, with her daughter on her hip, voiced her appreciation for delivering her baby. Mr. Jonsson hobbled up with his gout. Drake couldn't eat for the interruptions. Almost everyone in the room was a patient he had seen at one time or another.

A grizzly-looking man came to stand in front of Trice. He watched her. Said nothing. It took Drake a moment to recognize him. Drake had last seen him when he was a teenager. Even then it hadn't been but for a moment or two when Drake helped him out of the clinic.

She glanced at Drake, then looked at the man again. "Can I help you? Is there a problem?"

"I am Olafur Bjonsson."

Trice went statue-still, then jumped up and cut around the table. Drake hurried after her. He feared she might scare the man off.

Drake came to stand beside her, putting out his hand. "Mr. Bjonsson. Thank you for coming. I would like you to meet Dr. Beatrice Shell. As I said in my message, there is a chance you are related to each other."

Trice looked as if she wanted to throw her arms around the man. Her eyes glistened. Was she going to cry?

Olafur continued to study Trice. Then he grunted. "She looks like my aunt, Lilja Andresson, who ran off to America when I was a child."

Trice stared at the man. Her mouth opened, closed and opened again. Finally, she found her voice. "Can we talk sometime? Please. I would really like to get to know you. Learn about your family. Possibly mine."

He nodded.

"Thank you so much. I promise to call you."

Olafur nodded again, then walked away.

Trice hugged Drake. "Can you believe it? I really might have family."

He smiled indulgently. "It is wonderful. I wasn't sure he even got my message. I hated to leave when you had not made contact with him. I never imagined he would show up here."

"I can hardly wait to talk to him. I'll call him

tomorrow. Do you think he has any pictures?"
Her words were tumbling over each other.

"May I make a suggestion?"

"Sure." She watched him, all smiles.

Drake gave her an earnest look. "I would be careful not to overwhelm him. Go slow and easy."

She took a moment before she spoke. "You're right. I'll be careful. And go slow."

Another person came to speak to him. When that person left, he and Trice returned to their seats. People continued to stop and speak to him, give their thanks.

Trice said, "It must be gratifying to know you have meant so much to so many people."

"It is."

The mayor joined them on the other side of Drake and drew his attention away from Trice. Drake would have rather spent his time with Trice. This would be their last night together. He was too aware of time slipping away. If he wasn't careful, he would become melancholy.

He had spoken to the surgery program leader in London that afternoon. They were expecting him in three days. He had just enough time to get settled in a leased flat.

Drake had eaten little of his food when the mayor stood and tapped on his glass, calling the place to order. "Quiet, please. I have a few words. Drake Stevansson was born and raised here. He went off to college and medical school and returned to help us when we were in desperate need of a doctor. Now it's his turn to go off again and succeed in his training as a surgeon." He looked at Drake. "We are thankful you put your life on hold for these past two years for Seydisfjordur. I don't know what we would have done without you.

"In appreciation, we've all contributed to this gift wishing you the very best." The mayor handed Drake a thick envelope. "Use this to help with whatever you need."

Drake's throat had a knot in it. He worked to swallow. He was overwhelmed with the generosity. He stood. "I don't know what to say. This wasn't necessary. It's too kind. I've enjoyed being your doctor. I will be leaving you in good hands with Dr. Shell."

The entrance door burst open. In a frantic voice, a man yelled, "There's been an explosion at the cannery!"

Trice was right behind Drake as they exited the door. As he passed the mayor, he thrust the envelope back into the man's hand for safe keeping. He called over his shoulder, "Trice, go to the clinic and bring anything you think would be needed in an emergency. Just fill any bags you can find. We can send others after them. Then bring my bag." With that, he picked up his pace, leaving her behind.

Ahead of them, gray smoke billowed from the cannery located on the fjord on the other side of the airport. The blue sky framed the plume of smoke.

She ran to the clinic, wishing for more stable shoes than the ones she wore. Throwing open the door, she hurried down the hall to the supply room. She picked up a large duffel bag and began dumping gauze, antiseptic and tape into it. Soon she had almost cleaned out the supply bins.

She took a moment to pull on Drake's shoes, which she had already borrowed once. With as much weight as she could carry, she started toward the door.

A man entered. "Drake said to come help you. I have a truck."

She thrust the bags at him. "Take these. I'll get the others. We're going to need blankets."

"People are gathering them. We should have some when we get to the cannery." The man headed out the door.

She returned to the supply room and picked up more supplies. With those in the truck, she climbed in the passenger seat.

The driver sped around the harbor. He honked the horn, clearing the people so they could get past. Three minutes later, they were traveling through the iron gates of the long red building.

Before the truck driver could pull to a complete stop at the front door, Trice had opened her door. She yelled, "Drake."

Another man loped up to them. "He's around this way."

"Hey, I need those two black bags on top," Trice stated.

The man reached over the side of the truck and grabbed the bags. Seconds later she was following him into the dim light of the building.

People were running around every which way.

"He'll be up these stairs in the boiler room." The man indicated the metal steps, and putting down the bags. "I'll go back for the supplies."

Trice hurried up the stairs. The area was almost dark. "Drake?"

"Here."

Relief filled her at the reassuring sound of his voice. She hurried forward.

"Trice, be careful. There is debris on the floor."

Her toe caught on a piece of metal. With luck, she remained upright. She kept moving. Finally she just made out the shape of Drake.

She dropped their bags beside him, then joined him on her knees. "How many people injured?"

"Ten that I know of. There are still eight missing." The pain of loss rang clearly in his voice.

She gave him an anxious look, grateful he was still in town for this event. She could have handled it, but she was glad to have his help. "What do you need me to do?"

"I need you to organize triage. Send four men to me with blankets. I'll have them carry some people out and lead the others. Set up triage as far away from the building as possible in case something is unsteady. So far, I've seen mostly minor things and breathing difficulties."

Trice stood. "I'll get started now." She turned away, then back again. "Drake. Be careful."

"I will." He refocused his attention on the man he cared for.

Trice hurried back outside. She found the man who had driven her. "I need you and three more men to go to Drake. He needs you to bring patients out here. I'll be setting up the triage area." She looked around her. "Over there in the parking lot for the injured. Bring them to me."

"Will do." The man called other men's names and headed inside.

A group of women came up to her. One said, "What can we do to help?"

"I'm setting up a triage station in the parking lot. I need the supplies in the back of that white truck and all the blankets you can find." Trice went to work seeing about the men and women Drake sent to her.

Marie, the nurse from the night of the dance, came to Trice. "What do I need to do to help?"

"See this patient gets oxygen." Trice moved on to the next patient. "This one needs stitches." She called to Marie. "Those—" she pointed to

the patient's right side "—will have to wait. She
will need to be moved to the clinic."

"A hospital has been set up in the community
center. There are a few who live here with some
basic medical skills. They are working there. She
will be well taken care of until you or Drake can
see her again." One of the women who had been
helping Trice waved a man over. He loaded the
patient in the back of a truck.

Trice liked being a part of a community who
came together during a disaster, no matter how
large it was. The people didn't wait on one person
to make all the decisions. They saw a need and
jumped in to fill it. This was the type of place
she would like to call home.

Trice quickly assessed the next man's broken
hand. Marie joined her. "This one needs his hand
wrapped until we can x-ray it and set it."

The next man lay on a blanket.

"Where does it hurt?" Trice asked.

"My foot. Part of the tank fell on it."

Trice pulled his pants leg up to see the man's
calf, which had started to swell. "Your foot is
most likely broken. Leave it in the boot, which
will give it support. We will set it later." She
waved to one of the men helping. "Over here."
The man stood above her and the patient. "This
man needs to be put with the group who need
an X-ray. Do not remove his boot. Understood?"

The man nodded.

Trice returned to see patients. The next had a superficial injury to the ankle. She left him for Marie to bandage. Thankfully the patients coming in were slowing. Since they had eased, Trice sent Marie to the community center to organize it and listed who needed to have care first. She also made lists of those who should be sent home after she or Drake saw them and people who needed attention overnight.

One of the men who had been helping Drake hurried up to Trice. "Drake needs your help inside. Can you come now?"

Fear went to her throat. "Is he okay?"

"Yes. He has a patient he needs help with."

Trice snatched up her bag. "Show me."

Drake hated to call Trice into such a dangerous situation, but he had no choice. He needed her assistance. He couldn't do this without her. Even then he wasn't sure they would manage to save the man's life.

"Drake. I'm here. What can I do?" She moved as fast as safety would allow.

He turned the flashlight on the man crushed between a large boiler and a beam.

"Oh, Drake. Is he still alive?"

"He is. I'm treating him for shock. He needs a blood transfusion." His voice held concern.

"Do you know his blood type? I'll start typing blood and getting more donated." She would see to that as soon as she returned to the outside.

"I'm going with O. I already have some of the men rounding up people."

"Send them to the clinic. I'll see about it," Trice assured him.

"The problem remains that if moved, he may bleed out. He would never make it to Reykjavík. He needs an exploratory laparotomy immediately if he even has a chance to survive. It needs to be done here and soon."

She placed her hand on his arm. "You can do it."

"There is no theater. No one to put him to sleep. No recovery."

"We'll use one of the exam rooms. I'll assist along with Marie."

"Marie?"

"She's at the community center, overseeing it. You have the skills. Use them."

Drake didn't have a response to that statement. Wasn't surgery what he had been wanting to do? But under these conditions?

"You stay with him." She placed her hand on his shoulder. "I'll go to the clinic and get things ready. I'll let you know when to bring him."

"There isn't much time." His look met hers.

"We'll hurry."

Time flew by and crawled at the same time as Drake waited to hear from Trice. His patience was almost gone by the time the blood came. He had spent the time regularly checking vital signs and rigging a system to deliver the blood along with helping the cannery workers form a plan to move the huge boiler.

When a man arrived with two pints of blood Drake immediately went to work administering it. It would be too little too late if Trice didn't hurry.

His phone rang. He put it on speaker, needing both his hands for his patient.

Trice's voice said, "Drake, we'll be ready for you when you get here."

"We're on our way." He hung up the phone. "Okay, guys. Let's go to work." With two men on each side of him to lift his patient, he directed the man on the crane. "Lift slow and easy."

The groan of metal made him fear they might be damaging the man further, but they had to get him out. Not soon enough, the space opened so the men could pull the injured man out.

"Slowly. Lay him on the blanket." Drake managed the blood still flowing. Trice had better have plenty of blood waiting at the clinic. They would need it.

They made it out of the building without a mishap. Waiting near the door sat a truck with the motor running and padding for the patient in the back. The men placed the patient on the bedding, and Drake climbed in beside him. To the driver he said, "Keep it slow and steady."

Trice was waiting for him at the clinic door. She rushed to meet him when the truck stopped. "How is he doing?"

"Just hanging on." Drake jumped from the back of the truck.

"You go get scrubbed in, and I'll see about prepping him. Everything you need is lying out in the restroom." She went to work overseeing the unloading of the patient.

Drake glanced into the first examination room. It was filled with furniture. The next one had the door closed. He continued to the restroom. Just as Trice had said, a gown, surgical hat and gloves waited.

Minutes later, he opened the door to the examination room. It had undergone an obvious makeover. Everything that was unnecessary had been removed. He could smell a hint of disinfectant. No doubt Trice had made sure the walls and equipment had been sanitized.

A gurney sat in the middle of the room with his patient on it. A tray with instruments stood beside it. The examination light had been positioned near the bed. With two swift steps, he stood beside the man. He pulled on his headlamp. It felt good to have it on again.

"I located what gas I could find to use to put him to sleep." Trice wore surgical gear as well.

"I went through your office and found your surgical headlamp."

Behind her stood Marie.

"We are ready when you are, Doctor," Trice announced, taking her position on the other side of the patient from him. Marie stepped up beside him.

"Vitals, please," he said.

Trice rattled them off. "He's being given blood now."

"We need to get him to sleep." Drake picked up the gas mask and placed it over their patient's face. "Trice, monitor vitals."

Her gaze met his. She nodded.

Confidence he wouldn't have said he possessed filled him. He could do this in this makeshift theater. He had excellent support.

"BP is ninety over sixty," Trice announced.

"That's to be expected with internal bleeding. But it's time to stop that. Let's find those bleeders. Scalpel."

Marie placed it in his palm.

Slowly and carefully, he made a midline incision in the man's abdomen.

"Suction?" What were they going to do for suction?

Marie handed him the end of the tube to the stomach pump machine. He looked at her. "It was Trice's idea."

His gaze met Trice's. The woman never ceased

to amaze him. He went to work removing the blood pooled in the man's middle section. "We're going to need more blood."

"It's on the way. People all over town are giving." Trice moved to check the transfusion site.

There was knock at the door. A voice called, "Blood is here."

Trice went to the door to take it. She returned to hook it up to the man after checking the IV.

Drake searched the internal organs. "I wished we had a way of taking X-rays."

"You don't need them." Trice's voice held complete confidence. "You'll find the problem."

He suctioned the area as well as he could. "Sponge."

Maria handed him one. "Keep count. We don't want to leave one lying around somewhere. In fact, keep a written tally."

"There's a pad and pen in that drawer." Trice point to the small cabinet in the corner.

Maria found it and made a notation.

Drake couldn't believe what Trice had managed to pull off in less than an hour.

She had created a full operating theater. He couldn't think of many situations more dire than doing surgery with rudimentary equipment in an examination room turned theater in a remote area.

"We need to find the bleeders or bleeder and get him closed. The helicopter will be here in a few hours after we know he is stable enough to move to Reykjavík. Suction." He cleaned the area as well as possible once more. "Sponge. Trice, vitals."

She rattled off precise and to-the-point numbers.

"Now move the spleen aside and let me see if the bleeding is from there." He searched the area. "There is one. Clamp."

Maria handed him something close to what looked like a surgical clamp.

"What is this?"

Trice spoke up. "A hair clamp. I couldn't find any surgical clamps anywhere. I had to improvise."

"Nicely done." She was wonderful.

She had a smile in her eyes.

"Let's get this stitched up and look for more. Marie, you handle suction. Trice, you help with holding the two sections together while I stitch."

Both women went to work.

It felt good to command a theater. There was no room to argue with the man's life in the balance.

Marie opened a suture kit and handed him the needle already pre-threaded. She suctioned. With the area clear, he carefully joined the two ends of the vessel. "Hold it right there, Marie. Almost done. Suction."

"Excellent. Got it." He nodded to Marie.

Blood still pooled in the man's cavity.

"We've got another somewhere." He went looking, gently moving organs around in a mythical order. He lifted a lobe of the liver. "There it is. This is going to be tricky. Vitals."

Trice gave him the numbers.

"Okay. He's holding his own. Marie, I want you to hold the liver like this." He positioned it where he wanted it. "Trice, I need you to clamp this off the best you can." He held the vessel. "Then help keep the area clear so I can see and get it attached. We're going to have a devil of a time because of the angle."

They all took their positions, and Drake went to work. It might have been the most rudimentary of theaters and the job the most difficult he'd had to perform, but he did some of his finest work.

He stepped back. "Suction one last time. Marie, count those sponges. We can't afford an infection or left behind sponge."

Trice and Marie followed his directions while he searched for further issues.

"Well done. Let's close. Any broken bones will have to wait until he can be x-rayed." Drake checked his watch. "The evacuation helicopter should be here in an hour. We couldn't ask for better timing."

In a silent room, he closed the man's abdomen. While Marie covered the man in blankets and checked his vitals every fifteen minutes, Trice and Drake cleaned the room.

Trice said, "You've got some skills with stitches."

"I practiced long enough." He grinned behind the mask. "Marie, thanks for your help. You go get some rest. You've done a night's worth of work," Drake said.

"It was amazing to watch you. Both of you. Trice will make a great local doctor. I'm glad I'll be working with her. I going to check on those injured at the community center before I get some rest."

Trice pulled off her gown and hat. "Thanks for your help. You were amazing. You've earned a rest. I'll see about the community center."

"But—"

"I've got it. If you want to, you can come in later today and oversee what's going on. And Marie, thank you. I wouldn't have wanted anyone else's help."

"Thanks. I feel the same about you." Marie smiled and headed for the door.

With her gone, Drake said, "Apparently Marie has become one of your fans as well."

"An emergency helps people see others in a different light. Plus, I think she knows something is going on between us."

Drake would agree with that.

Trice finished putting away supplies. "I've got to go now. I need to check on things at the community center. I'll have work to do in the morning."

"I'll be right here until the evac arrives." He stood over the patient.

She hesitated at the door. "Don't you have to leave this morning?"

Her sad eyes were almost his undoing. "I'm postponing for at least twenty-four hours. I can't leave you with all this to do by yourself. You've got your hands full."

"We had some last night together."

It wasn't what he had planned. "Story of my life. There's always something getting in the way of my plans."

Trice gave him a quick kiss on the lips. "I'll check the other patients. After you see this patient off, why don't you go to my place and get some sleep? It's closer than yours, and you'll be nearby in case you're needed."

"You'll join me?"

His hopeful look warmed her heart. She nodded. "As soon as I can."

Trice trudged to the community center. Exhausted, she still had work to do. In the two weeks she'd been in Seydisfjordur, she'd done more, felt more than she had in her entire life. She wasn't sure she could keep up this pace, but she was exhilarated by the idea of seeing if she could.

Here in this remote place, she'd found herself.

A place to belong, a place to grow, and place she could call hers. If only Drake stayed…

At the center, she entered to find patients lined up in orderly rows. One wall was a food area. "Good morning."

The women working there greeted her with tired looks.

"Would you mind fixin' a plate for Drake? I'm going to check on the patients here. Then I'll take it over to him."

"You have done enough. I'll see about that," the older of the two women said. "Thank you for all you have done for us."

"You are welcome. And thanks for taking a meal to Drake. I'm sure he'll be happy to see it."

Over the next hour, Trice reviewed charts and ate a bite herself. She heard the whirl of the helicopter approaching. Her and Drake's patient would be leaving soon. They had done good work together. Pretty amazing stuff in fact.

And the town. They had come together and organized as if they had practiced it. They knew each other so well, they knew whose skills to call on. Those who had some medical experience led those willing to help.

Trice told the lady who came in for her shift of overseeing care that she was leaving to get some rest. "Call me or send someone after me if there's the slightest problem. When I return, we'll see about discharging patients."

In the early sunlight, she walked home. The lights were off in the homes, and a few businesses were opening.

She was turning the corner of Luce's house when her door opened. "You did good last night. You okay?"

"I'm fine."

"You need to rest. He is already doing so." The old woman carried no censure in her voice.

"He'll leave tomorrow." Trice wasn't as good at removing emotion from her voice.

The old woman looked sad but resigned. "It has to be."

"I know."

"One must learn what they really want." Luce stepped inside her house and closed the door.

Trice had found what she wanted. Caring, support, and a place where she gave and got it in return. She'd found those here with or without Drake. She had also found love despite the fact it was leaving her. Her heart squeezed at the idea of losing him. Yet he had to go, just as she had to stay. He needed a chance to find what he wanted.

She opened the door of her home to find Drake sound asleep on his stomach in her bed. He snored softly. She went to the bath and showered. Pulling on an oversize shirt, she headed for the bed as well.

Giving him a shake, she said, "Scoot over."

She wiggled in next to him, pushing him to give her room using her behind.

Drake rolled to his side and pulled her to him. He murmured next to her ear, "Everything okay at the center?"

"Under control."

"Mmm."

A soft snore filled her ear. She snuggled into him. He would be gone in less than twenty-four hours. She would take what she could get for as long as she could get it.

Hours later, she woke to Drake nuzzling her neck while his hand under her shirt fondled her breast. "I'm sorry. I can't help myself." He nuzzled her ear again. "Reconsider us staying in contact."

Trice was flattered. She snuggled closer. She would miss this time and intended to absorb as much of it as possible. Trice didn't want to have this discussion now. She wanted him to make love to her. "We've already talked about that. I have responsibilities here, and you have training in London."

"I'll come here when I can. You come to me when you can. We can talk and write, call often."

She hated being the one to voice reality. "It won't work."

His lips followed her brow. "You won't even try?"

Trice kissed his chest. "It's not that."

"Then what?" He looked at her.

"I'm tired of having only half of what I want. I don't want crumbs. It's time I demand to have the whole cake. To be the center of someone's attention. To come first. You can't do that in London, and I won't ask you to stay here."

"Come on, Trice. It'll only be for a little while. If we both work at it, we can make it work. We can get through the year, and then we can be together."

Would that be what she wanted to do? She already knew what it was like to be anonymous. She liked being included in a knitting circle. The fact that people helped others without question. She had no desire to return to what she had before. No longer would she settle for part-time. Trice looked away.

"You think you belong here?" He pulled away and lay back on the pillows.

"I don't know for sure, but I believe so. But it's not all about Seydisfjordur. It's about me." She pointed to her chest. "Me standing up for what I want. Finding my place in the world."

"You don't think you can do that with me?" Drake growled.

"Not in London. Not when you are focused on surgery." She raised a hand before he could speak. "Which you should be. This was supposed to be a fling for a reason. I care too much for you to hold you back. I would never want that. You need to go. I won't hold you here. I can't."

"You sound like Luce. She pushes me to go, yet she knows I worry about her."

"I will take care of her. You need to go. If you don't, think of all the people who might not get the care they need. You owe it to yourself, and your future patients to finish your training."

All Drake's hurt showed in his eyes. Her heart broke. She hadn't wanted it to end this way.

He threw the covers back. "You finish getting some sleep. I'll go check on the community center and see if I can send some of the patients home. I'll be busy the rest of the afternoon tying up business and packing. Bye, Trice."

Through tear-filled eyes, she watched him dress, then walk out the door and out of her life.

# CHAPTER ELEVEN

TRICE DIDN'T SEE Drake for the rest of the day. She stayed busy at the clinic and then later at the community center. He had discharged a number of the patients at the center, but there were still others that needed to stay at least another day.

Day turned into night, and she returned home lonely and sad. She'd been both of those before. She would survive. She would work through them again.

By the time she went to bed, there had still been no word from Drake. More than once, she had thought of going to him. What would she say? That she had changed her mind. But she hadn't. She couldn't lead him on to believe that.

She wasn't surprised he was hurt, even understood it, but she knew what it was like to have promises made to stay in touch and then there be nothing. She didn't want that. Refused to live like that ever again. It was better to cut it off clean and remember each other well.

Trice wanted him to concentrate on his surgery. Getting his career started. To have his dream. Worrying about her wouldn't make that happen. He wouldn't intend to hurt her, but it would happen. Not once had they discussed forever. Had he even considered that?

Returning to her house, she tried to get some rest, but it never came. In a short amount of time, she had become used to sleeping next to Drake. Even that she would have to adjust to, and it might be the hardest to accomplish.

She couldn't figure out a way to make their situation different. For them to have a future, one of them would have to give up their dream. She wouldn't ask Drake to do that. His skills were needed. But she also couldn't agree to give up what she'd finally found—a community. Exhausted, she walked from the clinic to her house.

The next morning, Trice strolled to the front of Luce's house on her way to the clinic. Luce's front door opened, and the old woman stepped out. "He came by earlier to say goodbye. He left you this." She handed Trice a paperback book. "He said for you to keep it."

Trice had heard the plane taking off. She had hurried outside and watched as he circled over the town and headed south.

The older woman said quietly, "Drake needed to go so he can know his mind. His heart is here. He must learn that. Then he will come home."

"I'm sure he'll come back for a visit."

The way Luce looked at Trice told her the woman's words had another meaning. "You must work to stay busy. Time will go by."

Not fast enough to heal her heart.

"That way you will not notice him being gone." Luce patted Trice's arm.

Trice would notice Drake being gone no matter what she did. "Thanks. That's good advice." She would start today. Determined, she squared her shoulders. She walked to the clinic, went in and proceeded with business. She was here to do a job, and she would do it and do it well. She had her research to review and a call to Olafur to make.

Yet that heavy block of sadness and loneliness weighed her down.

Over the next week, he didn't call, nor did she receive a letter. She didn't like being cut off any more than she had the times it had happened before. Yet Drake was doing as she had asked.

Trice worked to fill her days, but her nights were long and sleepless. As the hours crawled into days and those into weeks, it didn't get any easier. She just pushed forward. Every time she heard the engine of a plane, her heart palpitated with the possibility it was Drake, then crashed when it wasn't.

Drake had circled Seydisfjordur the day he left. Had Trice looked up, hoping to see him one more time? Had she been as disturbed by him leaving her behind as he was by doing it?

He had studied the little town nestled on the water below him. It had been his home forever. He had gone knowing he had left part of himself behind. Trice might not still be in town when he did return, but he knew well the others who made up Seydisfjordur would be there just as they always were.

He hadn't liked the way he and Trice had parted, but he couldn't help his anger. She didn't even want to try to work out something between them. It wouldn't have been easy, but they could have tried. Her problem was she had no faith in anyone wanting her.

If they both wanted the relationship, they could have figured out how to make it work and overcome the complications. They didn't have to become part of the negative statistics that said it was next to impossible. She wanted stability. To be the center of someone's world.

Had he made her think she could be? No, he hadn't offered her that. Not once had he offered her anything permanent, especially with him. Drake blinked. Was that what he wanted? Trice in his life forever?

He had been gone for three weeks. He wished he could say he was happy and had adjusted well to returning to the structure of hospital schedules and the requirements of surgery. But that wasn't the case. Thankfully, his skills weren't lacking.

He disliked the noise and lights of the city. They were nothing like he remembered. Now they irritated him. He missed the quiet of a starry night. The peace of the wind.

To make matters worse, he longed for Trice. He couldn't get beyond that. Or that he had all but demanded everything be his way. That she come to London. That she work there. She would have been giving up everything for him. He'd been unfair to even think she might follow him when he'd seen how happy she was in Iceland. Above all, he wanted to see her happy. Yet what he'd asked for wouldn't have done that.

He had been so confident that when he reached London, he would be so caught up in his work that the pain of losing Trice would ease. That hadn't been the case. He had planned this move for so long, had looked forward to returning to surgery so much, that he shouldn't be this miserable. He was horribly lonely for Trice. And he missed Seydisfjordur.

He recognized happiness. He had it with Trice. What he felt now wasn't it. Still, this was what he needed to do, to hone his surgical skills. Then he could return to Iceland prepared to do more for his homeland than he had been doing. He just had to give his feelings time. To hope that it worked. He had made a commitment, and he would stick with it.

He had just finished his third surgery of the day. He had seen inside three humans' bodies, yet he couldn't say what they looked like or their names. He couldn't say what they did for a living, or how they had come to get a scar on their hand or what nickname their mother called them or what their favorite folk dance was. All of that he knew about most of the people in Seydisfjordur. His patients in the hospital were just people passing through the OR who he would never really know. He missed the personal connection of working in a small clinic.

*You do not know your heart or your place.* Hallveig's words marched through his head.

He did know now where his heart was, and his place as well. It was time he went home to Trice and Seydisfjordur. With that decision made, the weight he had carried on his shoulders fell to his feet. Finally, the center of his back relaxed for the first time since circling Seydisfjordur the last time.

An hour later, Drake said to the balding, stern-looking man standing beside him as they scrubbed their hands, "Dr. March, may I speak to you in your office after this procedure?"

The man observed him a moment and nodded. "That will be fine."

* * *

Drake sat in the chair across the desk from the older surgeon. "How can I help you, Stevansson?"

"Sir, I'm sorry to tell you this, but I will not be staying with the program."

The man sat forward. "And why not? We held a place for you. Why would you leave us after only three weeks?"

"Thank you, sir, for doing what you did, but the two years I've been gone have changed things. I've learned to appreciate knowing my patients. By name, not as a number. I love surgery, I do, but I need more. More interaction."

The older man leaned back in his chair. "Your work is impeccable, but I have to admit I've been unsure about your happiness with working in a hospital."

Drake wasn't sure how to respond, so he remained quiet.

"I realized how much you wanted to rejoin the program and how patiently you waited until you could, but you seem to go through the motions, which are better than par, but your heart doesn't seem to be in your work."

Drake sat straighter. "I assure you—"

The man held up his hand. "This is not a criticism but an observation. Please speak freely."

"Working in a large city just isn't for me anymore. I belong in Seydisfjordur." And with Trice.

"You're going to give up surgery to return to your small-town clinic? It will be a waste of talent."

"I'm sorry you feel that way, sir. But this isn't the right place for me. I'm sorry to have taken your time and a space, then let you down."

"There is no way to change your mind?"

"No sir, there isn't." On that Drake had no doubt. He was going back to Seydisfjordur and begging Trice to have him.

"Then I guess all I can do is wish you well." The man stood and offered his hand. Drake shook it. "I hope you aren't making a mistake."

Drake squared his shoulders. With complete confidence he said, "I am not."

As the days went by, Trice became less confident about having made the right decision regarding Drake. What she had was nothing. No phone calls, no notes, no interaction. She'd requested it be that way. He was honoring his word.

Yet everything in her mind, body and soul clambered to hear his voice, to know how he was doing.

Maybe he was right. They could compromise. She had only a year's commitment to Seydisfjordur. The town hadn't asked her to stay longer, and if they did, she didn't have to agree. Yet by then, how she and Drake felt could be completely different. Only she knew it wouldn't be for her.

Was he as lonely as she? She felt like Seydis-fjordur was home, but without Drake, she wasn't as sure as she had once been. She should be with him.

The only true bright moment in her life was when she had spoken to her potential cousin, Ola-fur Bjonsson, at length and requested a DNA test. She was waiting for it to return. Still, she felt deep in her soul it would be positive. He was her family. He had a sister who had three daugh-ters, but they lived on the other side of the island. Trice hoped to meet them one day. Just know-ing they existed filled her heart. She had blood connections in a world where she had never had anyone. Yet something was missing. Drake was the connection her heart longed for.

Would he even respond to her if she called? He'd been angry with her when he had left. How would he react if she dared to call him? Would he be glad she did?

One afternoon, she dared to call his number. Her heart almost beat out of her chest. Would he answer? Her heart settled into its place when the call went to voicemail. She sank to the chair while she listened to his voice. At the beep, she hung up. Tears flowed like they never had before. Maybe it was best to leave well enough alone.

Three days later, the sound of a plane made her head pop up from where she worked at her desk. Would she ever move beyond that reaction to a plane engine?

Since she didn't have any patients, she walked outside to the front steps. The sun shone brightly. She watched the plane circle, then line up for landing. The plane had markings like Drake's, but she knew that was just wishful hoping. The plane came to a stop near the terminal.

A man came around the front of the plane. His mannerisms reminded her of Drake. Hope had her imagining things. But the idea it might be him pulled at her enough to keep her standing there. The pilot looked her direction, but the distance was too far to really make out who he was. Still she stared.

The man walked toward the terminal. John, who ran the airport, met him and shook his hand. The man slapped him on the shoulder just like Drake would have. Trice slowly went down the steps and started walking toward the airport. She wanted to run, but controlled her actions, not wanting to embarrass herself if it wasn't Drake. Her heart quickened. What if it was him?

She started down the road. He moved so much like Drake, but he was in London doing surgery. Her feet kept moving of their own accord. Her pulse ran wild in anticipation. He walked toward her along the road around the harbor. The closer he came, the more he looked like Drake. She picked up her pace. His strides lengthened.

It was Drake!

She broke into a run. He loped toward her. He was close enough now for her to clearly see him.

He dropped the pack from his back and opened his arms. She ran as fast as she could the last few yards, not stopping until she slammed into his chest. Drake rocked back with the force of her reaching him. His arms tightened around her. Her arms went around his neck, and she clung to him. He squeezed her tighter. If it was up to her, she would never let him go.

They remained wrapped in each other's arms for a few minutes. Trice fought the moisture filling her eyes. She focused on absorbing the fact that Drake's heat warmed her, and he was there with her again.

"I've missed you." Her voice was gruff with emotion.

"I've missed you too." He sounded as if he were having a difficult time controlling his emotions as well.

She pulled away enough to see his handsome face. "I'm sorry I was so stubborn about us not having anything to do with each other."

"I'm the one who should apologize to you. I wanted everything to go my way." His look held nothing but sincerity.

She cupped his cheek. "I wanted you to have your dream."

"Honey, when you're in my arms, I have my real dream. I love you."

"Drake, I love you."

He kissed her, long and sweet and perfect. Her heart swelled. All her life she'd been looking for connection, roots, love. This man in her arms gave her all of that and more.

Drake picked up his pack and pulled it over one shoulder. He put an arm around her waist and directed her toward the clinic.

Trice slipped her arm around his waist, too, laying her head against his shoulder. "Luce said you would be back."

"Somehow Luce always knows."

"She seems to. Why are you here? How long can you stay?"

"Can't a guy say hi before you start grilling him?" He grinned. "Can't I just come visit you?"

She gave him a sheepish look. "I'm so excited you are here."

"Why don't we ride up to my house, where we can talk uninterrupted?"

She stopped and studied him a moment. "Because I don't think you have talk on your mind when we're at your house."

His grin turned wolfish, predatory. "Well, you might be right about that, but I'd like for you to come with me anyway."

"Let me close the clinic and put out the sign about where to find me." Trice hurried ahead.

A few minutes later, they climbed into his truck, which had remained parked behind the clinic. He had left it for her to use when needed. Drake drove up the steep, winding road to his house. He opened the front door, letting Trice enter first. He closed the door behind him, grabbed her and kissed her so tenderly she came close to crying.

He rested his forehead against hers. "I didn't want us to be interrupted at the clinic. Sometimes the town doesn't know boundaries."

"Drake, shouldn't you be in London? Is something wrong?"

He gave her another deep kiss. "Everything was wrong. You weren't there. I came home for you."

Her eyes narrowed. "For me?"

He cupped her cheek. "Yes, for you. Sit. I'll explain."

Trice wasn't confident she would like what was to come, but she did as he requested. "I need to say something."

He sat beside her, but not close enough for her to touch him. His look turned earnest. "I gave up my surgery fellowship. I want us to be together. I'll do whatever it takes to make that happen."

Trice wanted to wrap her arms around him but remained where she was, her hands tightly clasped together. Her voice turned stern. "Drake, I won't let you give up your dream. You are a surgeon. You should be doing surgery. What you love."

"I love you more." He pulled her into his lap.

Placing her hands on his chest, she pushed back so she could see his face. "I don't want you to one day resent me because you gave up something you love for me."

"That will never happen. You are the most important thing in my life."

She searched his face. "We can make it for a year writing, seeing each other over the internet, visits."

"I want more than that. I want us to really be together. Right here." His eyes were bright with the possibility.

"How?" Her brows rose.

"I'm back here to stay." He grinned.

"But Drake, you can't to that. You were born to be a surgeon. I hope you didn't leave for me."

"I left for me. And because what we have together is more important to me."

"I can come to London after I finish here. We can find a place outside of the city where we can have the best of both worlds."

He studied her with a look of amazement on his face. "That's not what you want. I know you well enough to know that."

"I would do it for you. I could make it work."

"I don't want you to make it work. I want you happy. This is your happy place. It is mine as well. I have found it has a hold on me no matter how much I might try to say it doesn't. No matter where I am, it will always be here, calling me. With you here, it screams, *I belong here*. One of many things I have learned lately is that I can be invaluable wherever I am. It just may not take the same form."

She kissed him. "It took you long enough to figure that out."

He smirked. "Some of us are slow to get the idea."

Trice cupped his cheek. "Yes, they are." She dropped her hand. "If you come back here, I will need to find a job elsewhere. I won't be needed."

"I'm not coming back to take your job. I was already packed and ready to head this way when a representative of the Reykjavík Hospital phoned. He wants me to start a pilot program for local surgical clinics. The first one would be right here. I would handle the simple surgeries and emergencies as needed in the surrounding area. I also discussed it with the town council through the mayor. I want to use the money they gifted me to help buy a small CT machine. They agreed. Iceland's medical commission hopes you would be willing to stay and oversee the clinic and continue to help me when your year is over. They heard how efficient you were when we did surgery."

It was almost too perfect. Trice appreciated the

excitement on Drake's face and how animated he was talking about the plan.

"We can be together. Right here where you want to be and where I have realized I belong."

Trice didn't know what to say, she was so overwhelmed.

Drake took both her hands. "What do you think? Would that make you happy?"

"That would be wonderful. I can't think of anything more wonderful."

"Nothing?" He watched her with a smile on his face.

"What's going on, Drake?"

He continued to look into her eyes. "This is a personal matter, not a medical issue."

"Are you sick?" She looked at him, suddenly concerned.

"I'm fine except for one thing. My heart hurts."

She sat forward. "What's wrong with your heart?"

"It hurts for you. I've missed you. I love you, Trice." He went down on one knee. "I love you so much. I know we haven't known each other long, but I also know I love you and I want to marry you as soon as possible."

She threw her arms around his neck, squeezing him tightly. "I love you too. I always will."

"So, what do you say?"

Drake looked so unsure, she had to take pity

on him. "Yes, yes, yes, yes, yes, yes, yes! A million times yes!"

He kissed her with such tenderness that expressed his love clearly. She sighed when he released her.

"I can get my family here in a couple of weeks," he said. "Do you think you could be ready to marry me by then?"

She grinned. "I bet I can call a meeting of the knitting circle and have it done in no time."

He threw back his head and laughed. "I'm sure you're right."

Her gaze locked with his. "One more thing. Having a family is important to me. I know you are good with children, but how do you feel about having some of your own?"

"If they're with you, I want them. In fact, I think we should start practicing right away." He took her hand and tugged.

In the doorway of his bedroom, she stopped him. She met his questioning look. "I came here hoping to find blood family, and I found so much more. You are the real family I've been looking for. Thank you for that."

"Honey, I'll always be here for you. Seydisfjordur has always been my home, but with you here, it's where I belong."

\* \* \* \* \*

# HARLEQUIN
### Reader Service

# Enjoyed your book?

Try the perfect subscription for Romance readers and get more great books like this delivered right to your door.

See why over 10+ million readers have tried Harlequin Reader Service.

## Start with a Free Welcome Collection with free books and a gift—valued over $20.

Choose any series in print or ebook. See website for details and order today:

## TryReaderService.com/subscriptions

RSBPA24R